INSPECTOR GHOTE TRUSTS THE HEART

INSPECTOR GHOTE TRUSTS THE HEART

H.R.F. Keating

CHIVERS LARGE PRINT
BATH

British Library Cataloguing in Publication Data available

This Large Print edition published by Chivers Press, Bath, 2000.

Published by arrangement with the author.

U.K. Hardcover   ISBN 0 7540 4225 1
U.K. Softcover   ISBN 0 7540 4226 X

Photoset, printed and bound in Great Britain by
Redwood Books, Trowbridge, Wiltshire

There is only one Commissioner of Police for Greater Bombay. So I would like to make it clear that the figure depicted in my pages as holding this office is in no way connected either with Shri S. G. Pradhan, occupier of that onerous post at the time of writing, or any other Commissioner.

INSPECTOR GHOTE
TRUSTS THE HEART

CHAPTER ONE

Inspector Ganesh Ghote looked quickly over his shoulder. No one. As far as he could tell there was no one in sight who knew him. This would be the moment.

'Sahib, sahib,' the new young beggar on the far side of the steps up into Bombay CID Headquarters called again. 'You are my father and mother. All I have is you. Give, sahib, give.'

And, despite the pleading tone, there was an underlying note of cockiness. Of happy certainty.

Ghote crossed the five yards of pavement in front of the steps and stood close beside the boy. Looking down at him as he sat he could see every detail of the withered right leg stretched out on the dust-engrained paving-stones. It was like the small branch of a dead tree, shiny with many careless brushings-by. A thing of no account.

'Why should I give?' he said to the upturned face beneath him. 'Many are giving to you already, and it is the start of the day only.'

'Sahib, none give, none. You are my father and—'

1

'Nonsense. I can see there are coins under where you are sitting.'

Abruptly the boy grinned, quite un-abashed, his eyes sparkling with dancing, cascading enjoyment.

Ghote pushed his hand into his trouser pocket and gripped with sweat-sticky fingers the wavy-edged two-paise coin he had marked out for just this purpose when he had taken up his money as he had dressed. It was the life in the boy that got him, as it had done every day for the past six weeks, ever since the lad had come to this pitch when its former occupant had died. He pulled out the two-paise piece and pressed it hastily, stealthily, into the boy's thin-fleshed, hard, little, expectant hand.

There. It was done.

Freed of a burden, he swung sharply away and prepared to mount the steps at a trot.

'Ah. It is Ghote. Inspector Ghote.'

A cold lurch of dismay froze him into stillness. Spotted. Found out. A hard-headed inspector of the Bombay CID seen falling for the totally transparent wiles of a mere boy of a beggar.

Slowly he turned round.

And it was worse, far worse, than anything he could have imagined. There standing on the pavement just beyond the beggar boy and

2

looking across at him with a cold, authoritative gaze was none other than the Commissioner himself.

Behind him, drawn up to the kerb, was the quietly magnificent car that is the privilege of the man who heads the Greater Bombay police force. Its driver sat, dark-capped and bolt upright, at the wheel. Its engine was purring softly as the workings of time itself.

'Yes, Inspector Ghote,' the Commissioner said, as if he was coming quietly and decisively to a conclusion. 'You don't look very much like a policeman.'

Ghote felt the phrase as being the final condemnation. And he saw that it was just, down to the last syllable. No, he did not look at all like a policeman. And could there be anything worse? It was his whole aim to be a policeman. And the Commissioner, there on the broad pavement barely three yards from him, standing with feet just apart, balanced, calm, was the very idea of the policeman carried to its highest point. The link that had been between them had in a flash become a yawning gap.

'Right,' said the Commissioner with quick authority.

This would be the sentence. Permanently condemned to work in Records? Sent away to the Traffic Department?

'Now listen carefully, Inspector. There's not a great deal of time. I've just had a most urgent telephone call from a personal friend of mine, Mr Manibhai Desai. His small son has been the subject of a kidnapping attempt. Thank God the men took the wrong child, the son of a tailor. But it looks as if they don't know they did, and in the note they left they threatened to kill the boy if Mr Desai got in touch with the police. But we must have a man in the house for when they make telephone contact, someone who doesn't have "Police" stamped all over him. So, Ghote, you're just the fellow.'

*   *   *

Less than two minutes later Inspector Ghote was sitting, small and crouching, alone in the back of the Commissioner's car. Ahead the enmeshed morning traffic of Bombay seemed to melt away before the high gleam of their polished radiator. In Ghote's ears the Commissioner's final words still rang. He had told him to take the car and had said that he himself would make arrangements for him to be relieved of all other work. And then, as he had ushered him in, holding the door open himself, he had made a swift parting comment.

4

'Inspector, this is a job that may well require the utmost tact. It needs a man of feeling. I saw you giving to that beggar boy as I drove up: I'm glad to find at least one of my officers hasn't let his duties rub away all the heart in him.'

A glow lit Ghote up from the inside like a warm lantern hung in the dark night.

But what of the task that awaited him when the big car's driver had brought him to the Cumballa Hill home of Mr Manibhai Desai?

He leant yet further forward and pushed to one side the smooth-sliding heavy glass panel that separated him from the driver.

'Tell me,' he said, 'do you know Mr Desai? Does the Commissioner visit him often?'

'Not very often, Inspector sahib,' the driver answered. 'I think I must have taken him about three times only in the past year. It is more a friendship of the memsahibs, I am thinking.'

Ghote thought he understood now why the Commissioner had come driving down to Headquarters. When a man is urged on by his wife, even if he is the Commissioner of Police for Greater Bombay himself, it is likely that he will go to extravagant lengths to appear to be doing what he is asked.

'And Mr Desai?' he said to the driver. 'What do you know about him himself?'

'He is the man who is making Trust-X,' said the driver simply.

It was all he had to say. Everybody knew about Trust-X Tonic Tablets. Trust-X was 'the tonic you owe to your loved ones'; everybody knew this from the big advertisements on the screaming hoardings, on the radio and in all the newspapers. And everybody, it sometimes seemed, acted on that call that could not be ignored and paid out for the sheets of tablets with those days of the month printed in scalding red against the pocket for each pill. Ghote bought them himself for his Protima. They cost him rather more than he liked paying and there were times when he dared to doubt that she really was less tired for taking them. But when one month's supply neared its end he always sent away for a new one, and if the solid, white, four-square envelope—'Trust-X comes to you under plain cover': what unspoken promises of sexual renewal—did not arrive in good time he always worried.

No wonder they were heading for Cumballa Hill and its great blocks of new luxury flats, centrally air-conditioned, surrounded by greenery, looking out over the blue stretches of the Arabian Sea. The man who had invented Trust-X was bound to be living in such conditions.

What were the other circumstances of his home life?

Ghote leant forward again on the firmly sprung seat of the Commissioner's car and addressed the driver once more.

'Mr Desai has many children?' he asked.

'The one boy only, sahib. He is aged about four. The mother died in giving birth, and two years ago Mr Desai married again. I believe the second Mrs Desai is younger than her husband. The burra memsahib is often saying Mrs Desai is like a daughter to her.'

'I see,' said Ghote.

Inwardly he felt a growing hollowness. Heavier burden than working directly for the Commissioner, it seemed he would be working directly for the Commissioner's wife.

'Did the Commissioner tell you any details about what happened at Mr Desai's?' he asked.

'No, sahib. Commissioner sahib told only that I would be taking an officer to Desai sahib. I am to stop some distance from the block, and not to say a bloody word to anybody whatsoever, sahib.'

'Quite right,' said Ghote. 'A business like this is invariably the work of a gang. It is well possible that they have a man, or more than one even, watching for signs of police

7

activity. They threatened to harm the boy if any such steps are taken.'

'And the tailor's son,' the driver asked, 'would they harm him instead?'

Ghote had already thought about this, and he found that all he could say was that he did not know. What would ruthless kidnappers do when they discovered they had got the wrong victim? Would they just push him out somewhere to join the four thousand children lost in Bombay each year? Push him into the streets, like a fisherman who has caught a fish too small for anyone to eat? Or would they kill him?

They might. They all too easily might, if they believed he would be able to give them away. Because they would know that, once they had lost the hold that the possession of the son of a rich and popular man gave them, then the full might of the forces of the law would be out against them. One thing is vital in police work when a case of kidnapping occurs: to show that it does not pay. The actual taking of a child is seldom really difficult, so that, once the notion gets about that the much more complicated business of getting a ransom sum and remaining undetected can be achieved, then there will almost certainly be a spreading outbreak of this cruellest of crimes. So that it is a matter of the utmost importance to apprehend with speed any set of criminals who embark on the business. And such men would well know this.

Which meant that the chances for the little son of the tailor must be slim. But, on the other hand, kidnappers soon realize that it is bound to blunt the hunt afterwards if they keep strictly to their share of a bargain and return the victim promptly in exchange for the stipulated sum. And this means that they take every precaution to prevent that victim while he is in their possession from being able to tell where he is hidden.

If these men felt that they had taken sufficient precautions, perhaps the chances for the tailor's boy would be reasonable.

'I think this would be a good place to set you down, sahib,' the driver said. 'It is the penthouse in the next-after-this block of flats. Mount Greatest it is called.'

★   ★   ★

Stepping out of the steel-walled express lift that had swept him to the fifteenth floor of the upthrusting, pink-hued luxury block, Mount Greatest, Inspector Ghote hurried across a wide and well-cared-for marble floor to the front door of the penthouse, a rich span of glossy oiled teak. He put his finger on the bell-push that occupied its dead centre above a wide stainless-steel letter-box.

The door opened startlingly at almost the instant he touched the button. Ghote found himself confronted by a tall, broad-shouldered man with striking features, deep-set eyes, a wide mouth slightly parted to reveal large and even teeth, a crisply pointed, jutting chin and, most prominent of all, a thrusting, stallion-nostrilled prow of a nose. Only a touch of grey in the well-groomed, wavy hair and a thickening at the waist showed this was not a vigorous thirty-year-old but a man into his fifties. He wore European clothes, a silk suit cut with evident dash, a dazzlingly white shirt and a broad, flowing and colourful hand-printed silk necktie.

And he grasped in a thrust-forward right hand a large revolver.

'Mr Desai,' Ghote said quickly, in no doubt this was the opulent, benefit-conferring inventor and manufacturer of Trust-X. 'Mr Desai, I am police.'

Manibhai Desai kept the big revolver pointing still at Ghote's stomach.

'What is your name?' he demanded.

'Ghote. It is Ghote. Inspector Ghote, CID.'

10

Abruptly the revolver swung round beckoning Ghote in. He stepped across the threshold and the proprietor of Trust-X promptly slammed the wide teak door behind him.

'It is as well for you I had your name already,' he said. 'If I had thought you were one of the swine that tried to take my Haribhai I would have shot you down like a dog.'

'But it is possible you would have shot some harmless visitor only,' Ghote said.

'They must not stand in my way,' Manibhai Desai declared, his stallion nostrils flaring.

Ghote mustered all his authority.

'Please, at least to put the gun in your pocket,' he said. 'It is most important at the present juncture to pay the utmost attention to any telephone calls incoming. And if there is a danger of firearms discharging that would not be possible.'

Mr Desai pushed the big revolver into the pocket of his dashingly cut suit as if it were red hot.

'Please,' Ghote said in alarm, 'you must apply the safety-catch. Otherwise you would be in considerable danger.'

As vigorously as he had jammed the revolver into his pocket Mr Desai now

11

yanked it out and feverishly examined it.

'Perhaps you are not greatly acquainted with the use of firearms,' Ghote suggested. 'Kindly allow me.'

He reached forward and succeeded in removing the big pistol from Mr Desai's dangerous grasp. He glanced at it. It was an Enfield .380. Not much to his surprise he saw that the catch had all along been in the safe position.

'Why should I be a first-class expert on guns?' Mr Desai demanded aggressively. 'I am not a goonda. I am a businessman. I have worked my way in the world by providing fine quality service to my fellow men, not by shooting and killing and inflicting severe flesh wounds.'

'No, no, of course you would not be expert,' Ghote answered. 'But perhaps, as you are not, it would be better if I were to retain this weapon while I am here on the premises.'

'Yes, yes,' agreed Mr Desai. 'But if those damned swine show their faces, you will kill them, yes?'

'You can trust me, sir,' Ghote said, putting every bit of emphasis at his command into the double-sided declaration. 'But please also show me at once where is your telephone. It is of the utmost importance I hear what these anti-socials have to say.'

'There is a phone here,' Mr Desai answered. 'But there are others too everywhere in the flat. Will you listen on one extension while I am speaking on another?'

'No,' Ghote said. 'I do not think that would do. It is important that I am beside you to give advice. We will have to act to our level best to make them supply details in full. The greater the extent of our knowledge, the better police would be able to deal with the fellows.'

Instantly at the mention of the kidnappers Manibhai Desai's deep-set eyes blazed again.

'The dogs and sons of dogs,' he shouted. 'They must be caught. Hung by the neck. To dare to try to take from me my Haribhai. To dare.'

'They will not be caught unless I am hearing full details,' Ghote said a little sharply.

The tall manufacturer of Trust-X subdued himself with an effort.

'Very well,' he said. 'I will tell. Everything took place first thing this morning. Every day my Haribhai goes down early to the garden beside the block to play. He loves to be in the open air. He loves to run.'

He jumped round with total suddenness and strode over to a far door, thumping on it

13

sharply with his fist.

'My Haribhai, my Haribhai,' he called out with strident anxiety. 'He is there? He is safe?'

A woman's voice answered. Ghote could not catch what it was she said because of the thickness of the door between them. But, whatever it was, it seemed to reassure Haribhai's father. He came back and flung himself down on to a round, squabby, modern-looking chair upholstered in a bright orange, that stood beside the table on which, Ghote saw, the telephone rested.

'Today,' Manibhai Desai resumed, 'the tailor was here. We need new curtains. New curtains everywhere. The sun bleaches them so up here.'

Ghote glanced across at the large window of the hall through which indeed the morning sun was streaming, fresh and brilliant up at this height above the dust of the city. The curtains were of a rich, golden-yellow velvet. He was unable to see much sign of bleaching.

'The tailor,' he asked, 'it is his son that they have taken?'

'Yes, yes,' Mr Desai answered, with a wave of his large hand. 'That is the boy. The tailor, you must understand, visits often. There is a great deal to be done always. My wife is most insistent to keep right up-to-date. The most

14

modern, straightaway. So very often it is necessary to have the tailor here. And he is a widower or something, I do not know. But in any case he has the habit of bringing his boy, who is aged about five, with him.'

'The two little ones became friendly?' Ghote asked.

'No, no, no, not at all. Not at all. My son to be a friend for the son of a tailor only? It is not possible.'

'But they were together when it happened?'

'Yes, yes. Playing together. They were playing together.'

'I see.'

'No, no. You do not at all see. You do not understand what happened.'

'But then what did occur, please?' Ghote asked, blinking a little.

'That is the bloody part about it. The two of them had changed clothes. When my son came screaming back to his ayah in the garden to say that some men in a car had driven away with Pidku he was dressed in Pidku's clothes. I have had to have them burnt.'

'Burnt? But they might have been of help.'

'You can never tell with the clothes of the poor. There might have been disease, insects, anything. They had to be burnt *ek dum*.'

'I see,' Ghote said. 'But tell me more, if you please, about exactly what happened. Your son had gone down to the garden to play under the charge of his ayah, and the tailor's son was with him also. How did the boys come to change clothes?'

'I do not know, I do not know. My little Haribhai would not want to wear poor clothes like that. An old T-shirt only, no doubt secondhand or even worse, with a picture of a ship at sea on it, and trousers that were torn in the back part. Always he has the best clothes, latest fashion, straight from the shops as soon as they come in.'

Ghote thought it was plain enough why rich little Haribhai had wanted to wear the T-shirt with a picture of a ship on it. In a few minutes he would have to get a description of the 'latest fashion' clothes that Pidku, the tailor's son, had been wearing when he was taken. But Haribhai's father would not be the one to ask for that. For a really meticulous description the ayah would be the one to approach.

'The ayah?' he asked now. 'Why was she not watching your son? She has been questioned?'

'Questioned she has been and tears she has wept. But she will say only the boys went a little way away as often they did. She is

16

locked up now, and my chauffeur is guarding.'

There was a note of firm satisfaction in Mr Desai's voice. Ghote decided that, with the telephone perhaps about to ring at any instant with the call from the kidnappers, the ayah could be left in her unofficial, and illegal, imprisonment for a little longer.

'Did she say why she was not watching?' he asked.

'She says she was talking with the ayah of the Mehta family,' Mr Desai answered. 'They live in one of the flats down below. They have three little girls only.'

'I see. And so the two boys wandered away. No doubt, if as a sort of joke they decided to change clothes, they would want to go somewhere where they could not be seen. Where was it that they went?'

'There are bushes,' Mr Desai said with dark gloom. 'I will insist they are chopped down. Today.'

'And your son? Has he been able to tell what happened?'

'Yes, yes. He is a talker among talkers, my Haribhai. You should hear him order the servants. What a voice. I could not do better myself.'

'And he said what?' Ghote asked, with a touch of sharpness.

'That two men came and offered sweetmeats from their car. My Haribhai went. I suppose because that little devil of a tailor's boy was going. The men then offered ride in car, and again the same thing. Only a short way along the service lane at the back they stopped car and pushed my son out. Then they drove away. Top speed. And it might have been my Haribhai that—'

And then the telephone rang.

CHAPTER TWO

Ghote gave a convulsive start and flung himself on the telephone where it stood, a softly gleaming white instrument, on its table. He lifted the receiver and clapped a hand across its mouthpiece.

'Say "Hello" only,' he instructed Manibhai Desai, now sitting upright on the edge of his orange tub chair as if his tall body had been injected suddenly with a frame of steel.

Ghote held the receiver towards the manufacturer of Trust-X and carefully raised his palm from the mouth-piece. Mr Desai swallowed.

'Hello,' he said, hardly succeeding in choking the word out.

Ghote snapped back his protective hand. The two of them listened like hovering kites.

'Is that you, Manibhai?'

The voice was unmistakable: the Commissioner.

Ghote handed the receiver over to Mr Desai and stood respectfully back. A sharp inquiry spluttered from the far end of the line.

'Yes, yes, he is here. We are waiting for those swine to ring up—'

19

Another splutter from the far end.

'Yes, yes. I will try. I will do my utmost to keep quite calm, but when I think—'

Splutter, splutter.

'Yes, he is here beside me. I am handing over.'

Ghote took the receiver.

'Inspector Ghote here, sir.'

'Well, what do you make of it?'

It was almost a man-to-man inquiry. Ghote straightened his stooping back.

'Here in the flat, Commissioner sahib, it is a question only of waiting for them to ring us. Everything must wait for that. But I have been worried by the problem of witnesses at the scene of the crime, sir.'

'What's the trouble there?'

'Sir, the kidnappers' approach appears to have been made via a back lane adjacent to the garden of the flats here. It is very much possible that there were witnesses to some stages of the proceedings at the very least. But it would be a matter of deploying a considerable number of personnel to locate such witnesses, and you can see the danger there, sir.'

'Policemen all over the place, yes. No, Ghote, we must avoid that for the time being certainly.'

'On the other hand, Commissioner sahib,

witnesses will forget, and they will also add to what they remember with every quarter-hour that passes.'

'True enough, true enough. But it is a risk we must take. My wife—I myself will not hear of Mr Desai's boy being put in jeopardy if it can in any way be helped. You may say that you had my authority.'

'Very good, Commissioner sahib. Thank you, sir. I will ring off now in case those fellows are wanting to call.'

'Quite right, quite right.'

Ghote replaced the white telephone receiver on its rest with a sense of holy awe.

'Well,' he said to Mr Desai, 'we must only wait and wait. But you have more to tell. There is, for instance, the note the miscreants left. Where is that?'

'It is here, here.'

Manibhai Desai plunged his hand into his jacket pocket and produced a single sheet of coarse-looking, yellowy-white paper.

'It has been in your pocket all the time?' Ghote asked. 'You have put it in and out? Have others handled the sheet also? Was there an envelope? Where is that?'

As the implications struck him he felt a growing sense of shock. This was evidence, solid fingerprint evidence perhaps, that had been so carelessly handled. Manibhai Desai's answer to his blurted questions confirmed his worst fears.

'If there was envelope it has been thrown away. What good is envelope? It is what they have written here, here, that matters.'

And a long forefinger jabbed and jabbed again at the coarse sheet, adding no doubt two more well-defined, obliterating fingerprints to those already there.

'How many others have read besides yourself?' Ghote asked hollowly.

'But many. Of course, many. Do you think my wife would not want to see what the swine have written? Do you not think that all those in this household who love my little Haribhai would not want?'

'Then since the sheet is covered already with finger-prints,' Ghote said, 'I might as well just take also.'

'Fingerprints, fingerprints,' Mr Desai said, suddenly horror-struck. 'Will they be saying I rubbed out the fingerprints of those sons of dogs?'

'It cannot be helped,' Ghote replied wearily, as he plucked the sheet out of Mr Desai's hand and read the brief message written on it in crude capital letters of red crayon.

EF YOU WAT SEE YOR SON ELIVE DO NOT TEL PELICE—WET BY

TELEPHONNE FOR MESSEGE

And then at the bottom of the sheet again, in more urgently scrawled letters: DO NOT TEL PELICEWALAS

Ghote considered. Not much really to help there. Too few words altogether. Of course, they indicated that the men had enough education to be able to write, and that they knew a bit of English. But in Bombay almost anyone with daring enough to conceive a plan of this sort, and with the ability to select as a target a person like the proprietor of Trust-X, would have these skills. And down among the criminal classes there would be thousands, perhaps even as many as ten thousand, who would come into this category.

No, a lot would depend on the telephone message. When it came.

And it was plain, too, that the kidnappers, whoever they were, had been well aware in advance of what the police reaction would be. They must have realized very clearly that theirs was a crime that the forces of order could not let go undetected.

When they were caught, if they were caught, there should be material enough here to make sure of a conviction. Plainly the men were not the sort to know much about handwriting. It should be easily possible to get a good expert into court to state that this

23

was their writing, even with these rough capitals. And there might too be some fingerprint evidence, once the writer of the note was in police hands to be checked, even if the chances of finding clear enough prints now to tie up with a file at Central Fingerprints Bureau were almost certainly hopeless.

He carefully placed the coarse sheet in his shirt pocket and buttoned the flap.

And then his engrained conscientiousness made him ask one more question, though he knew such a pernickety attitude was not going to be popular with the forceful Mr Desai.

'Please,' he said, 'where exactly is envelope now?'

Manibhai Desai, his bold-featured face still visibly affected by the thought of what his blunder over fingerprints might mean in failure to bring to justice his son's attackers, sat with broad shoulders drooping on the little orange tub chair and said nothing in answer.

Ghote looked at the white telephone. If it were to ring at this instant his awkward line of inquiry could be postponed. The telephone sat on the gleaming, laminated mock-rosewood surface of the table, impersonal and cold, as if it was merely some small object whose use was not immediately apparent.

Ghote cleared his throat as loudly as he could.

'The envel—Please, it is necessary that I should examine the envelope also.'

Manibhai Desai darted him a glance of quick fury. Such looks, Ghote, realized, would in other circumstances send many a senior employee of Trust-X Manufacturing into a cold slide of fear about his continued chances of employment.

'What are you bothering with this?' the proprietor of Trust-X barked. 'At any moment the telephone will be ringing and we would be able to take a hold of those filthy swine. What are you bothering with other matters altogether?'

'It is a question of the possible disposal of the envelope,' Ghote said lumberingly. 'You told it had been thrown away. In very modern flats of this type there is often, I understand, waste-disposal unit in operation.'

'Of course, of course,' Mr Desai agreed. 'Are you thinking we would not have such appliance?'

Ghote's heart sank. The envelope, he felt certain now, would contain some clue to who the kidnappers were.

'Please,' he said, 'while we are waiting would you be so good as to carefully consider whether the envelope was put in such a machine?'

'It was thrown away, thrown away,' Mr Desai replied with tetchy vagueness.

'But it might constitute valuable clue,' Ghote burst out.

'Clue? Clue? What clue could there be in an envelope only? A brown envelope of poorest quality?'

Ghote's brain flew round. And he could think of no single answer that would not be ridiculous. If the note's fingerprints had been obliterated, then the ones on the envelope would be doubly so. And was it likely that the kidnappers had meticulously put their name and address on the envelope's back? Or how could a letter left at the scene of an abduction bear a postmark?

'Well,' he said slowly, 'in a matter of this sort you can never tell what might be revealed if a very close examin—'

And then the telephone rang.

Before Manibhai Desai had time to answer the call himself Ghote snatched up the white receiver, clapped his hand over its mouthpiece and issued his instructions in a fierce whisper.

'Say "Hello" only.'

'Hello?'

There was a moment's silence. Their straining ears could detect the insect-clicking murmur of the open line. Then a voice spoke.

'It is Mr Trust-X?'

His hand firmly over the mouthpiece again, Ghote hissed out more directions.

'Say "Yes" but ask also "Who are you?".'

'Yes, yes. It is Manibhai Desai speaking. But who are you, you filthy, child attack—'

Ghote contrived to slide his taut fingers obliteratingly across the front of the mouthpiece. He darted a glance of cold reproof at Mr Desai.

The telephone was silent. They both looked at the white receiver. At last Ghote could stand it no longer.

'Tell them you are listening only,' he ordered.

'I am listening,' Mr Desai uttered clearly into the mouthpiece.

'You had better listen well,' the voice answered immediately.

Ghote attacked it with every instinct of analysis he possessed. What class of person was it? It was a man certainly. But young or old? What sort of an accent was this English in? A Marathi one? A Gujarati? A Hindi? A Southern accent?

'Say you are ready to hear what he has to

27

tell,' he whispered.

'I will hear what you have to tell.'

'Follow this, Desai. We have talked to the kid. We have found out he is not your son.'

'Then you dirt—'

Again Ghote had to push his fingers over the mouthpiece.

'Ask something,' he said. 'Ask something. Ask anything. Ask who they think the boy is.'

'Who are you thinking the boy is that you have got?'

Mr Desai sounded every bit as authoritative as Ghote could wish. The voice at the far end was silent for a moment. Then it answered.

'Pidku. Tailor's kid.'

That and no more. Not nearly enough to work on.

'Ask for proof.'

'What proof are you offering for this?' Mr Desai duly demanded.

'Just be listening,' the far voice came back.

No characteristic accent. Almost certainly above the age of, say, twenty. Uneducated. Flat.

The voice, apparently satisfied that the proprietor of Trust-X was listening, resumed.

'We are making no difference in our

demand.'

'What? What is that? What are you saying?'

'For Haribhai we would have to ask twenty lakhs of rupees,' the kidnapper stated flatly. 'For Pidku, same money.'

The manufacturer of Trust-X stood blank with shock. Ghote, equally striving to adjust himself to this utterly unexpected new situation, hissed a flurried, snatched-at direction.

'Tell that you want time.'

'No,' Mr Desai flashed back at him.

'Yes, say it,' Ghote countered, putting all his force into the words. 'Say it. Say it. They must at least be made to talk more.'

Mr Desai looked at him, his deep eyes hot with mutiny. But then a shake of the head indicated reluctant agreement.

Ghote took his hand off the mouthpiece.

'Listen,' Mr Desai said slowly down the line. 'Listen, please. It is not possible to decide a thing like this straight-away. You must give time. Will you ring again?'

'In one hour. And no police, or we kill. Okay?'

And with a click of finality that struck like a blow in the tense silence of the luxurious hall of the penthouse the receiver at the far end was put down.

For almost half a minute neither Ghote nor Manibhai Desai spoke. Ghote was appraising the great stark fact that the mystery caller had planked down in front of them. He hardly could face thinking about it, so big and brutal did it seem, but rather he approached as near it as he dared, snuffling nervously at its odour. He thought, at one irrelevant moment, that no doubt the proprietor of Trust-X, for all his accustomed incisiveness, must be feeling exactly as he did.

To demand the enormous sum of twenty lakhs of rupees. It would be enough to pay for, say, a whole fleet of one hundred fine cars. To demand all that, not for the return of a precious son, but for the restoration to another father of his child: it was a stroke of world-reversing magnitude.

Would Manibhai Desai pay? Would he even think of paying? What would he himself do if he were asked to pay every last paise he possessed to save the child of a stranger? Yet how could one not?

He had been staring, as had Mr Desai, at the white telephone ever since he had slowly cradled the receiver at the end of the call, but now, very quietly, he stole a close look at the beneficent dispenser of Trust-X.

The tall businessman's strongly-marked features were becoming moment by moment

30

locked more and more in a mask of not deciding. It was plain to see. His wide mouth below the stallion nostrils was growing more and more fixed in a straight line of saying nothing. His deep-set eyes were retreating instant by instant further and further into inward-turned seeing nothing. Gradually but inexorably he was cutting himself off from everyone and everything.

Suddenly Ghote felt he must make contact with this vanishing mind while there was still some faint chance of doing so.

'Mr Desai,' he said.

His voice was unnaturally loud in the quiet. The proprietor of Trust-X started violently.

'Mr Desai,' Ghote repeated. 'What are you going to do?'

'But—But—' said Manibhai Desai with a vague feebleness that, Ghote guessed, he had perhaps never shown in his life before.

And then, visibly, he pulled himself together and produced his answer.

'Nothing,' he said. 'I am going to do nothing.'

He turned sharply away from the table and its telephone.

'Please do not mistake,' he went on. 'I am not saying that I refuse totally to pay any sum for the return of this boy. But at present no decision of any sort is necessary. There is one hour remaining before even the next contact with that swine on the telephone. What to do in that hour is for you to decide, Inspector.'

Ghote felt the weight settle evenly across his shoulders like the great wooden yoke across a broad bullock's back.

'That is so,' he assented. 'That is so.'

He straightened himself up.

'Very well,' he said. 'First we must make arrangements to deal with the next call the fellow makes. Luckily now we have a certain amount of time. One hour is not long, but it ought to be long enough to set up arrangements for tracing the call when it is made. The important thing then will be to keep the fellow talking and talking. But we will discuss that later. First, the arrangements.'

And he picked up the receiver of the white telephone again and dialled the number of CID Headquarters.

★   ★   ★

It took Ghote more than three-quarters of an hour to complete the arrangements for having the penthouse telephone line monitored. In the intervals of waiting to be put through to yet another of the extraordinary number of people it proved necessary to contact he worked out for himself a considerable list of delaying devices which the proprietor of Trust-X could use when, at the end of the kidnapper's hour, the telephone would ring again. He also reported once more to the Commissioner at his private residence, and once more regretfully advised him that any attempt to round up witnesses of the actual abduction must still be postponed as it was perfectly likely that one or more of the gang were watching the block for any signs of police activity. For the same reason he did not ask to have any help: he would have liked to be merely one of a team—perhaps simply the man deputed to search for that missing envelope—but even the thought that looking after his own mental comfort in this way might bring about the death of the tailor's son was enough to make him expel the whole idea from his mind.

But at last his long series of calls was over. He turned to Manibhai Desai, who during the whole of the time had been striding up and down the penthouse hallway, his eyes staring into some unseen distance.

'Mr Desai,' he said, 'as perhaps you have heard, full arrangements have now been made to intercept, and if possible trace, the incoming call. But tracing is by no means an easy matter. Therefore it is most important for you to follow my instructions with the utmost care.'

He was relieved to see that Manibhai Desai was actually paying him attention. He had feared that the proprietor of Trust-X would refuse even to talk under the ever-growing pressure that the kidnappers' monstrous transferred threat must be exercising.

But something else was nagging too, something that had been at the back of his mind all the while he had been so busy on the telephone. He brought it forward now.

'But first, before I tell you about the call,' he said, 'what about Pidku's father?'

'Pidku's father?' Manibhai Desai replied, as if Ghote had introduced some involved complication he could not even begin to grasp.

'Yes,' Ghote said sharply. 'Has he been told, the tailor? Does he know that his son is at least safe for the time being?'

Manibhai Desai did not reply.

He stood where he was and glared across the hall, as if perhaps he had detected a particularly outrageous piece of bleaching on the heavy-hanging yellow velvet curtains of the window.

'He is waiting in the flat?' Ghote asked, leaning forward a little towards the withdrawn face looking down at him and putting the hint of a crack into his question like the curling tail of a whiplash.

And the tiny edge in his voice had its effect.

'Yes, yes, I suppose. He was here when Haribhai came back. He would still be .. '

In the middle of this explanation the proprietor of Trust-X swung abruptly round, crossed the hall and hammered again on the door he had called through shortly after Ghote had arrived.

'My Haribhai?' he shouted. 'He is there? He is safe?'

This time Ghote caught the faint answer coming through the thick teak.

'He is playing only. With his radio-controlled helicopter.'

Ghote strode across the hall in Manibhai Desai's wake and tapped him briskly on the shoulder.

'Pidku's father,' he said. 'Please to call for him to come here.'

The proprietor of Trust-X turned. His deep-set eyes blazed in anger. Ghote wondered whether he was going to be struck.

But then, surfacing through the glitter of the ire like a timid night-animal putting its head from its burrow in a lightning-storm, something else appeared in the tall

35

businessman's demeanour. It expressed itself almost invisibly, in a slight sag of the broad, flung-back shoulders, in a hint of a perplexed frown on the high sloping forehead. It was submission.

Slowly, almost as if he had to wade through a tank of oil, he went over to another door leading off the hall, opened it and called out.

'*Koi hai?*'

The prompt sound of bare feet slapping on a stone floor answered. But before any servant appeared the proprietor of Trust-X called again.

'Tell the tailor to come. *Ek dum. Ek dum.*'

For a little they waited. Then to break the feeling of constraint Ghote began to tell Mr Desai what he should do when the kidnapper's next call came, how he should first let the telephone ring as long as he dared and then how he should not answer but leave it to him himself to take the call in the guise of a somewhat stupid servant. But at this point Ghote gave up. It was plain Manibhai Desai was not taking in a word.

They waited in silence a little longer.

Then the sound of hesitant steps came to them from the far side of the still open door.

'Tailor? Tailor? It is you?' Mr Desai burst out in a release of impatience so swift that it sounded almost like fury.

36

'Sahib, it is me.'

He came into the hall, swivelling round the post of the door like a battered old crab from down on the beach, victim of innumerable undertows, wearily rounding a rock to face of course danger, the only unknown thing being what form this time life's assaults would take.

He looked perhaps sixty, though Ghote guessed it was likely in fact that he was a good ten years younger. He was small and stooped a little, though probably he was taller than he appeared since his spindly legs were considerably bowed. He wore only a dhoti, its once gay check faded with washing after washing, and an old white singlet with a large, breathtakingly neat darn right over the middle of the chest. Steel-rimmed spectacles, clamped low on his nose, had their left-hand lens, which was cracked, mended by a wide strip of heavily yellowed transparent tape.

He brought his gaze to a point somewhere just above the top of Manibhai Desai's beautifully-hung, grainy silk trousers.

'Sahib?' he asked.

CHAPTER THREE

Both Manibhai Desai and Ghote stood looking at the stooping, spindle-legged figure of the tailor. Here was a man burdened already, Ghote thought, with the knowledge that once more in a life filled with troubles he had been dealt a thudding blow. Wantonly, for no good reason, his small son had been snatched away to somewhere totally beyond his reach. But, standing by the door post, looking inquiringly at the faintly billowing midriff of the proprietor of Trust-X, he had yet to learn that a new body-blow was about to be delivered.

He was, for all his troubles, Ghote saw suddenly, still really unscathed. And so he would be until he was told that men who seemed to be without scruples had demanded for his son's life the enormous sum of twenty lakhs of rupees.

But he had been summoned to be told just that. And he had come with quickly deferential obedience, and had dared to put that polite question 'Sahib?'

The question now had to receive its answer.

The proprietor of Trust-X noisily cleared

his throat.

'You—er—will be wanting to know about your son,' he said.

'*Ji*, sahib.'

As much as to say 'If it pleases you for me to want to know, certainly I will want'.

'Well,' Manibhai Desai said with fatherly heartiness, 'we have received a telephone call from these fellows.'

He paused.

'*Ji*, sahib,' said the tailor after a little.

'Your son is safe,' Manibhai Desai said.

Again a pause. The tailor could hardly be seen to react. Yet Ghote thought that in a tiny movement of the eyelids behind the spectacles with the transparent-taped lens he had detected a small gleam of hope which had been allowed to take fire, though ready to be extinguished at an instant should the enemy make as usual a new appearance.

Manibhai Desai turned away from him.

'By the way,' he said, with a forced casualness that would have been ridiculous were it not terrible, 'by the way I had forgotten to tell you who this gentleman is. He is a police officer, specially sent by my friend the Commissioner, to take charge of events. He also heard the call from that man.'

The tailor directed his gaze towards Ghote, raising it a little above midriff level, to

39

somewhere near the upper chest. He folded his hands in greeting and inclined his grey head.

For a little nobody said anything. Then Ghote felt obliged to urge the looming situation one centimetre nearer the edge.

'These men now realize that it is your boy that they have,' he said. 'Your Pidku instead of Mr Desai's son.'

'Sahib, I am sorry.'

And it was totally clear that the old man was not sorry because his son had been taken instead of little Haribhai Desai, but that he was condoling with the proprietor of Trust-X for the attempt made on his heir.

Ghote coughed. Once and harshly.

'Unfortunately,' he said—at once cursing himself for the dreadful formality of the word—'unfortunately these men are not at present prepared to release Pidku. In the circumstances.'

Again there was a silence. The tailor waited. This time Ghote turned towards Manibhai Desai. He swung on his heel so that it was perfectly plain he was putting the burden into the rich man's unwilling hands.

'Yes,' said Mr Desai eventually. 'Yes, it is a very regretable situation. You must see, the truth is—'

He stopped. The truth was too terrible to

tell.

He turned and put out a glance of pure entreaty. And the piteousness in it, coming from a man not an hour ago armour-plated against all the blows of life, moved Ghote. He took a deep breath and faced the old tailor.

'It is very bad news,' he said. 'They have demanded a sum of twenty lakhs against the life of your son.'

It was out. It was said. The both-arms blow to the head had been delivered.

The tailor quailed visibly under it. His bow-legs actually sagged by half an inch. His shoulders lurched forward.

And then he spoke.

'Twenty lakhs is too much.'

He said it in acknowledgement of a fact, an immense fact. It was as if he was stating that, yes, the Himalayas are there that, yes, the River Ganges flows, that, yes, the sea is deep.

Twenty lakhs of rupees is too much. Faced with that sum, there is nothing to be done.

The bare statement finally penetrated, as perhaps nothing else could have done, the layers of cushiony apathy that the dispenser of Trust-X had been wrapping and wrapping round himself ever since the flat voice on the telephone had made its outrageous demand.

He took one, quick, instinctive step towards the bent form of the tailor. His hands rose a little, open-palmed, as if he really had it in him to embrace the hunched shoulders of the pre-bereaved father.

'It—it is not so bad,' he uttered.

He stood looking at the victim, his bold-featured face showing the passage of conflicting emotions like rival armies spurring at night across a craggy countryside.

And then the sudden flood of impulsiveness was conquered.

'But it is not time to give up hope,' he said in a more controlled way. 'There is much that can be done. Inspector—er—Inspector—'

He tried to find the name with an extended, groping right hand.

'Ghote,' said Ghote.

'Yes. Inspector Ghote is a specially-sent, top-notch officer. You can rely on him to do his utmost. These fellows may still be apprehended. Yes, you have a top-notch man here, definitely top-notch.'

Ghote summoned up his resources to appear to be as much as possible the man Mr Desai had described. Perhaps it would comfort and sustain the tailor to think that his son's fate rested in the hands of a top-notch officer.

But all the alertness and force he contrived to put into his expression did not seem to make the least effect on Pidku's father. He

42

had stated his position. 'Twenty lakhs is too much.' The blow had been struck. All he had to do now was to suffer.

He stood in silence, looking down at the rich Mizrapur carpet on the polished floor of the hall.

'You have other children?' Mr Desai asked abruptly. 'Other sons? Fine boys?'

Ghote's mind, tenderized by the scene up to now as if pierced with a hundred needles, quivered thwackingly at the appalling crudeness of Manibhai Desai's questions. But all the same he was glad they had been asked. He wanted to know the answers.

And he wanted them, passionately, to be happy answers. It was too much to hope that the tailor would prove to be one of those men who father children as carelessly as they acquire items of clothing. Already he had shown that Pidku's loss—and this is what he totally believed it to be—was a blow to the heart of hearts. But could it not be that he had other children, and above all other sons, to assuage over the months ahead the bitterness?

'Sahib, I have no others. Many times did my wife give birth. To sons and daughters. But they were not ever to live more than a few days only. All except Pidku.'

'But—but—' the manufacturer of Trust-X

answered this blank challenge. 'But—Listen, I will pay. If it comes to the worst, I will pay. Something. At least something I will pay. A big sum. A good big round sum I will pay.'

Ghote supposed that at this the tailor should have broken down, embraced the feet of the manufacturer of Trust-X and poured out a stream of heartfelt thanks. In a film, he reflected, this would have happened—except that when the tailor had mentioned his dead wife it would have been the cue for a flashback to his early married days and, naturally, a song.

But this was life, and the tailor simply went on staring woodenly down at the floor in front of him.

'I will pay, I will pay,' the manufacturer of Trust-X repeated, his voice rising to a sort of shouting bark. 'Listen, I too have a son. An only son. And his mother died in giving him birth after many miscarriages. I know what it is.'

His strong features were glossy suddenly with sweat.

'And my wife now will not have,' he added inconsequently.

The extent to which his voice had risen under the strain of emotion was abruptly proved. The door on which he had twice hammered demanding reassurance on his

Haribhai's safety was suddenly thrust open and a woman who could only be his second wife came in upon them like a squadron with banners charging.

She was wearing not a sari but bright, cherry-red kameez and salwar, the cut of the tunic emphasizing with its clinging closeness the youth and litheness of her body, the tightness of the trousers at the calves pointing up the length of her slim legs. Her hair was fashionably cut and curled in a close cap round her considerably made-up face. The red of the clinging kameez was picked up and sent cascading out in so many sparkling drops by the cherry-bright varnish on her long, spiky fingernails.

'What is happening? What is happening?' she burst out.

Manibhai Desai turned away from the bent-shouldered, bow-legged figure of the tailor and summoned up a teeth-flashing smile.

'Things are coming under control, coming under control,' he said. 'We are getting somewhere.'

'And it is about time,' his wife shot back, sending a bright-with-anger glance darting round the hall.

Ghote, surveying the room in its wake, found that already the tailor had gone. He

45

must, he thought, have slipped back round the corner of the door like the cautious old battered crab that he was, hearing the impact of a possible enemy on the dense wetness of the sand.

'But my Haribhai,' Manibhai Desai said, with a returning edge to his voice. 'You have left him unguarded?'

'Guarded. Unguarded. He is in his room in the middle of the flat,' his wife answered. 'Who is going to do anything to him there? And if he must be guarded why cannot Ayah guard? That is what she is paid for.'

'But she is the one who must have betrayed my boy to those swine and sons of swine,' Manibhai Desai shouted.

'Betrayed? Betrayed? Ayah, has not enough sense in her head to think of betraying,' Mrs Desai countered. 'Am I not knowing her since I was a baby, since the days when my father was alive and we had money for ayahs?'

'Yes, yes,' her husband agreed, with quick soothingness. 'You have known her since you were a girl, and I dare say there is nothing in this business of suspecting her.'

'Then there is no reason for me to stay and stay in the flat,' his wife announced, a bright fire of triumph in her eyes. 'Were you forgetting this is the day for the Beat

Contest?'

But it seemed that Manibhai Desai did not even know what she was talking about.

'Beat Contest? Beat Contest?' he asked dazedly.

'Today,' Mrs Desai said, jabbing out the word. 'Today. At the Shanmukhananda Hall. Beat Contest. In aid of Bihar Flood Victims. With first prize generously donated by Trust-X Manufacturing.'

'Ah, that, that. I had forgotten. Yes, it is the day for that.'

'It is almost past the day for that. The show was beginning at 9.30. The Busy Bees are playing. The Atlantics also. Vibration and the Mini Beats. And then also there is—there is—'

A quick frown appeared on her smooth forehead at her not having the name on her cherry-red, cascading fingertips. But then she got it.

'Yes, yes. The Immortals. That is a first-class group. And there is also the Apaches. All are playing, and am I to be so late I will hear none?'

Manibhai Desai stood where he was and considered her demand to leave. Ghote felt that it was a considerable tribute to the crushing effect of the tailor's tragedy that he was pausing to think at all. In all but the most exceptional circumstances, he suspected, Mrs Desai would have her way in family affairs as an absolute matter of course.

Certainly she looked daggers now at not receiving immediate agreement.

And, within a second or two, her husband did in fact give in to her.

'Yes, yes,' he said. 'I suppose you had better go. Perhaps after all Ayah can guard Haribhai. But she is not to go out. She is not to go out.'

'Very well, you can tell her to stay in. It is all the same to me. And you will tell Ajit to get the car?'

In obedience to her request Manibhai Desai went across to the door through which the tailor had disappeared. But before he reached it he was unable to resist putting his tormented heart on display to her.

'Car and car you shall have,' he said. 'Have while you may. Soon it may be that we shall not be running two cars. Not even one perhaps, when I have answered the call on my resources.'

At least Mrs Desai rose to the bait, though instead of the gawping pond-fish her husband had hoped to catch he got a flashing shark.

'What call on your resources is this?' Mrs Desai demanded. 'Those men have not taken Haribhai. How can you be having to pay?'

48

'But they have taken the tailor's boy and for his life they have demanded the same sum,' her husband explained.

The flashing anger did not leave Mrs Desai's face.

'But if they have demanded a sum for the tailor's boy,' she retorted, 'then it is for the tailor to pay.'

'But it is twenty lakhs they have asked,' Mr Desai replied.

For a moment the hugeness of the sum gave his wife pause. She stood stock still in her figure-hugging red kameez and looked at him.

At last she spoke.

'Twenty lakhs,' she said. 'Twenty lakhs, and you were talking of paying. You would have trouble to raise twenty lakhs even for your cute little Haribhai. Don't be a fool, Mani. Don't start being a fool now.'

And she swung away, twisted at the knob of the wide front door, tugged it open and marched out.

Her husband stood turning his gaze from the back of the door to the spot before him where, not long before, the old tailor had quietly disappeared. Then at last he rallied himself, stepped to the doorway and in a series of loudly shouted orders arranged for the chauffeur to drive his wife to the Beat

49

Contest at the Shanmukhananda Hall.

But this display of squally energy seemed to exhaust him. He went back to the orange chair beside the telephone, slumped into it and stared with heavy despair at his knees encased in their knife-creased silk trousers.

Ghote imagined the balance he could not but be making between the wife he had taken after Haribhai's mother had died and the married life he had known before so closely paralleled from far below by the tailor's life.

The silence in the hall lengthened and lengthened. Ghote felt he must do something to break it.

He cleared his throat with a thin grating sound.

'There is the question of the envelope,' he said. 'The missing envelope, you know.'

Manibhai Desai looked up.

'She is not like that,' he declared as if in answer. 'You have seen her at her worst only. She is . . .'

He gave up. Ghote too gave up his not very convinced attempt to raise again the matter of the missing envelope, though something inside him had implanted the thought of it like a little irritating grain.

Again silence descended.

Ghote thought about the second Mrs Desai. Although at the moment she might not be appearing in the best of lights in her husband's eyes, it was certain that for most of the time those eyes must be dazzled by her. And they would be so again soon. It is seldom that scales drop in one flash of illumination, he acknowledged. So the chances of any money being paid out on the tailor's behalf must be much smaller now that Mrs Desai had declared so firmly against. Perhaps even they had ceased to exist.

This time the silence in the opulent penthouse hall did not last long. It was broken by the sudden shrilling of the telephone on the mock-rosewood table.

Ghote darted a look at his watch. Exactly one hour had passed since the kidnapper had ended his first call.

CHAPTER FOUR

The white telephone rang once, twice. Ghote had no doubt that it would be the flat-voiced criminal ready to tell Manibhai Desai where to leave the sum of twenty lakhs of rupees, probably in used 100-rupee notes—two thousand of them, it would not be too big a packet—in payment for the life of a five-year-old boy called Pidku.

For an instant, as the telephone shrilled out a third time, he was tempted to try to conduct the negotiations himself so as to have the opportunity of committing the manufacturer of Trust-X to making some payment for the boy. But he saw at once that there was no possibility there: the kidnapper would insist on talking to Manibhai Desai himself and no one else.

However, in accordance with their previously arranged plan, he did pick up the receiver and say, in a voice he tried to make thick with stupidity, 'Here is Shri Manibhai Desai's residence.'

'Get Desai, and quick.'

It was that flat voice, and it was in no mood to be trifled with.

Ghote put his hand across the mouthpiece

and turned to the manufacturer of Trust-X.

'It is the man,' he hissed. 'He is insisting at once to talk with you. I think you had better answer.'

He held the telephone receiver matter-of-factly out to Mr Desai.

If he could contrive that the proprietor of Trust-X would as a matter of course negotiate with the kidnapper, then perhaps the possibility of not paying any ransom at all, as Mrs Desai wanted, would simply not arise.

Manibhai Desai took the receiver.

'Hello?' he said.

Although he forgot to hold the earpiece away from his head, Ghote was able to hear the hard voice at the far end quite clearly.

'Listen, Desai. Here are your orders. And you had better obey. Go at midnight—'

'But wait. Wait. I cannot take instructions straightaway.'

Mr Desai was succeeding, with more acting skill than Ghote would have given him credit for, in sounding simply flustered. Were the people at the exchange really working flat-out at tracing the call?

But the flat voice banged back in, sharply as ever.

'Listen. Or you will be killing the boy.'

'Yes, yes, I am listening.'

Ghote, despite the tension, recorded an

53

inner leap of happiness. The manufacturer of Trust-X was after all still considering the fate of Pidku.

'Listen. At midnight go alone to a place we would tell. It would be where the beach comes near to a road, and you would walk down to the sea. There you would find a box painted white we have left between two rocks. Inside put twenty lakhs in old notes, fifties and hundreds. That is why we are telling now, to give time to get the notes. When you have left, next morning we would let go the boy.'

'But how do I know that?' Manibhai Desai snapped in.

'You will have to trust. We are trusting you. Trusting to say nothing to policewallahs. Wait for six tonight to learn just where to go.'

The voice ceased.

'Answer something,' Ghote hissed in Mr Desai's ear. 'Speak, speak.'

At all costs the line must continue to be kept open. The people at the exchange were certain to need longer than this.

'But— But, listen, please. I am not sure what time you said then. Please to repeat. Please, I insist.'

But even before Manibhai Desai had begun the line had clicked dead.

54

Giving Ghote a look of apologetic despair, the manufacturer of Trust-X put the receiver back on its rest.

Almost immediately the instrument rang again. Mr Desai snatched it up.

'Yes? Yes?'

'Mr Manibhai Desai? It is Superintendent of Police Karandikar who is speaking.'

Ghote experienced, willy nilly, a sudden stomach-turning sensation of rejection at hearing this name. Up to now he had succeeded in never having to work under Superintendent Karandikar, and he had felt always secretly grateful. The superintendent had an enormous and fearful reputation: he was, everybody always simply said, a tiger.

It was right, of course, that such a man should be given charge of a case like this. He was the obvious choice. Yet Ghote wished that chance had continued to keep him himself from coming underneath those claws. He knew that in an affair of this importance his own feelings must count for nothing, but he still could not help wishing, in a stream of pure desire, that it could be someone else now on the far end of the telephone.

He forced his uneasy stomach into quiescence and paid fierce attention to the small, incisive voice speaking sharply into Manibhai Desai's ear.

55

'. . . not in the least necessary. Appearing to treat with these people is a step that it may become proper to take in due course, but at present there is no need, no need at all.'

Ghote felt the beginnings of a slow, spreading sorrow. A man like Superintendent Karandikar, however, could hardly be expected to return anything but the hard answer to the kidnappers' demands.

'Very well, Superintendent, I shall take that advice,' Manibhai Desai said, in what seemed decidedly relieved tones.

But then he added a few words that marvellously halted Ghote's fast-deepening misery.

'Well, for the time being I shall do nothing, Superintendent. Nothing, for the time being.'

'You must not think of doing anything else,' Superintendent Karandikar's voice laid down firmly. 'Do not pay one anna's worth of attention to what those people say. They are not going to kill that boy.'

'Yes, but—' Manibhai Desai began doubtfully.

'I tell you, Mr Desai, so long as they go on thinking they may get money by threatening to kill the child they will go on keeping him so as to be able to threaten. Believe me, I know.'

56

Ghote, craning to hear that tinny tiger voice, found he could not totally agree with what it was saying.

He knew that the argument had been put forward before in kidnapping cases. And he could see that there was a great deal in it: if some evil men got hold of the child of a person of wealth, that child was more valuable to them alive than dead certainly. But, on the other hand, if they were at the start of a campaign of kidnapping, then they would have to convince all their potential payers that they were men of inflexible ruthlessness. And what better way could they have of doing so in this case than by brutally despatching little Pidku and then making sure that his body was found? The outcry that would follow would make any rich man pay all he was asked before even thinking of calling in the police.

And, of course, this was something that Superintendent Karandikar would undoubtedly have in mind. A series of successful kidnappings would bring enormous public and political wrath down on the police, and without rapid cooperation from the people under pressure it would be an almost impossible task to find the perpetrators. No, the superintendent could hardly be an unbiased adviser.

57

But how to put the other point of view to Mr Desai in face of that authoritative voice on the far end of the telephone line?

'Well, naturally, Superintendent, I shall give great weight to your views,' the proprietor of Trust-X concluded after the superintendent had added a few more pithy observations.

And, listening, Ghote allowed himself to rejoice a little. He knew that tone. It was the voice unyielding businessmen employed when they meant to keep their options open. He had heard it in a score of astute Marwaris, he had heard it in humbler circumstances from bania money-lenders keeping some would-be borrower on the hook.

It was a voice inflexible in its way as Superintendent Karandikar's own, and now that it had been used there was hope still of ransom for little Pidku.

'But I have my case to follow,' he heard the quick voice of the superintendent again. 'Kindly be so good as to put me on to my Inspector Ghote.'

My Inspector Ghote. Under the claws. Would he be able, if he had to, to summon up an inflexibility of his own?

He took the white receiver.

'Inspector Ghote here,' he said, as smartly as he could.

'Karandikar,' said the tiger voice at the far end.

'Yes, Superintendent? You are wanting progress report?'

'I am not. I am wanting to know why the hell the line was not kept open longer when that man was speaking. We missed him, you know. Missed him. And all because of your damned incompetence.'

'Yes, Superintendent. Sorry, Superintendent. But the fellow would not stay on the line, Superintendent. He simply—'

'I know just what he did, thank you, Inspector. I had a monitoring line set up just as soon as I was put in the picture. And I know the man ought to have been kept talking. By you.'

'Yes, sir.'

'Now then, I am told no effort has been made to pick up witnesses to the actual attempt.'

'No, sir. I thought—'

'On your advice, Inspector?'

'Yes, sir.'

'Then let me tell you that I am in charge of this case now. From here on it is a Karandikar affair. And you know what that means?'

'Yes, sir. No, sir.'

'It means action. Action, Inspector. Not

haverdavering about worrying whether looking for witnesses will cause trouble. It means going out after those witnesses and getting some good hard descriptions out of them. That boy was not taken by an army: at most they will be watching the block only. My team will be reaching the area in three minutes from now.'

'Yes, sir. And do you want me to—?'

'I do not want you to do anything, Inspector. You have been allowed to get your dirty little fingers into this case for far too long already. What I want from you is this only: at fifteen-minutes intervals you will send out from that flat one by one each and every one of the servants there. Starting with the ayah, for whom I shall need a 30-minute session. Right?'

'Very good, Superintendent.'

'They will proceed out of the block, turn left and walk down the road for two hundred metres. There they will see the shop of Rite-Wite Cleaners. I have taken over the premises, Inspector, and I will conduct interviews there myself.'

'Yes, Superintendent.'

'If after a lapse of thirty minutes precisely any servant has failed to return to the flat, you will pick up the phone and tell me. The number is 82 4835. I repeat 82 4835. Got it?'

'Yes, Superintendent.'

Ghote said the number over three times in his head.

'Then,' Superintendent Karandikar barked on, 'when all the servants have been dealt with you will request Mrs Desai also to visit me.'

Even before answering Ghote felt as if his stomach had been brutally hollowed away. He swallowed once.

'Mrs Desai is no longer here, Superintendent.'

'You let her go? You let go the most important witness we have?'

Ghote straightened his shoulders.

'Sir, she can be located if necessary at the Shanmukhananda Hall where she is attending Beat Contest. For flood victims, sir.'

'Very well, Inspector. We shall see. I will have a car over to King's Circle inside ten minutes. If they do pick her up, if, then you can breathe again.'

'Yes, Superintendent. And the boy, Haribhai, Superintendent? How are you going to arrange to interview him, Superintendent sahib?'

'A boy of four years only is not a witness in whom any reliance can be placed, Inspector. And now, put me on to Mr Desai again, and

61

then send that ayah down to the cleaner's at the double.'

'Yes, Superintendent. Right away, Superintendent.'

Ghote handed over the receiver of the white telephone with rapidity combined with deference, and waited while Superintendent Karandikar told Manibhai Desai that there was no need for him to take any immediate action over obtaining any money.

'We will deal with all that if it becomes necessary,' Ghote heard his incisive voice say.

Sickly he wondered what effect this final reinforcement of the superintendent's view would have on Pidku's fate. But the proprietor of Trust-X put down the telephone still preserving his rigidly non-committal attitude and Ghote breathed again.

Then he asked where the ayah was to be found, explaining Superintendent Karandikar's well-thought-out plan for holding the vital interviews with the servants without sending a whole squad of heavy-footed policemen into the flat. But Manibhai Desai had other ideas.

'Ayah cannot leave,' he said at once, his mouth setting in a long line of determination and his stallion nostrils widening in instant anger.

'But, Mr Desai,' Ghote urged, 'of all your

servants the ayah is most likely to have had contacts with these fellows. If you are wanting the threat to your son removed, then contact with these people is what it is vital to find.'

'Ayah is guarding Haribhai,' Mr Desai stated, with all the flatness with which he might impose a sharp increase in the price of the monthly consignments of Trust-X.

'But you have other servants. Cannot somebody else look after the boy for a short time only?'

'No.'

Ghote thought of Superintendent Karandikar waiting in the commandeered shop of Rite-Wite Cleaners. (How had he managed that? What a tiger.)

'But it is police orders,' he said. 'And it is in your own interests also. Why cannot, say, the tailor look after Haribhai for this short time only? He is used to boys of that age. That would be a solution.'

Haribhai's father gave a short laugh of contempt.

'That old man,' he said. 'My son would twist him round his finger like wet string only. And all the others also. If he wanted he would make them take him down the servants' stair to the gardens again. Only Ayah will resist him.'

'No,' Ghote said in abrupt contradiction, even somewhat surprising himself with his vigour.

Manibhai Desai's deep-set eyes glittered with sharp and sudden rage.

'No,' Ghote repeated. 'There is an answer. I myself will take charge of the boy during the absence of his ayah.'

He watched the answer hanging in Manibhai Desai's prow-nosed face. Would he come down on the side of fury, with the Commissioner invoked and no explanations accepted? Or would he come down on the side of the solution that would get things done?

Then he seemed to make up his mind.

'Very well,' he said, 'you will take charge of my son. But I am warning you he is not to be allowed to do just what he likes.'

He turned and led the way towards the door that he had hammered on earlier with feverish demands about his son's safety. And he added one other firm instruction.

'And I will not have you bullying him. He is my son, remember. He must do what he wants.'

Haribhai's room was a large and airy one looking out towards the sea, full and over-full of objects designed to keep the children of the wealthy in a state of contentment. But it was plain that, for all their number, size and cost, none of them at this moment was doing what it was intended to do.

The radio-controlled helicopter, which Mrs Desai had called out earlier was being happily played with, was now resting upside-down on its rotor blades, totally abandoned. What had evidently been not long before an immaculately drawn-up line of expensive toy vehicles had, it seemed, fallen victim to a series of hearty kicks. Each car was skiddingly scattered on the floor and the long thin control-wires with their little driving-wheels at the end were hopelessly tangled together. From a well-filled and neatly-kept toy cupboard three or four boxes had been savagely jerked out and their contents, mostly soldiers of the ceremonial sort—red-coated British Guardsmen, a Gurkha Band with tiny shining instruments, the US Cavalry with flags flying—lay scattered and intermingled.

The ayah, a dark-skinned hill-woman of perhaps sixty, dried-up but leather-strong, was tugging at an enormous rocking-horse that had been sent hurtling on to its side. They heard her expostulating as they entered.

'No, no, little sahib, no garden, no garden. Burra sahib says. Here to stay. To stay here all day. Terrible men. No, no, little sahib.'

Regardless of the arrival of the burra sahib and unkknown man, the little sahib responded with a glare of fury.

He was, Ghote saw, a plump child, even a stout one. But his father's strongly marked features could clearly be seen beneath the layers of fat that had been cherishingly applied by indulgent ayah and equally indulgent servants and father. And Ghote recognized too, with a fleeting, odd sensation of clarity, exactly that glance of prancing rage which he himself had been subjected to by Manibhai Desai not half a minute earlier.

'I will go out,' the little Turk was shouting. 'I will. I will. I will. Stupid horse. Stupid horse not to go fast. Stupid. Stupid.'

'What is this, my Hari?' said his father, striding towards him, dropping to his knees and putting a long encircling arm round his shoulders.

It did nothing to mollify the boy.

'Ayah will not come down to garden,' he declared. 'Stupid, stupid Ayah.'

'Yes, yes. She is stupid. But today is not a good day for garden. Today the bad men came and tried to take away my Hari.'

'Stupid bad men, stupid, stupid. Stupid Ayah.'

'Yes, yes. But Ayah is going now. Ayah is

going straightaway. She is to go out of the block, turn down the hill and go to Rite-Wite Cleaners. Now.'

It was an order of orders. The ayah began to ask why she was being sent on this unlikely errand. But the look of rage that father and son shared stopped her.

'*Ji, ji*, sahib, I go, I go,' she said.

And she scuttled from the room.

'Daddy will stay,' Haribhai announced, already looking happier.

'No, no, my little fighting man. Daddy cannot stay now. Daddy has much important work to do. But instead you are going to be looked after by a detective, a real detective from CID to look after my Hari.'

And, quick as a snake, the proprietor of Trust-X rose to his feet, slipped his arm away from his son and slid out of the room, shutting the door behind him with speedy firmness.

'Well,' Ghote said to his suddenly handed-over charge, 'what a lot of toys you have got. I too have a little boy, bigger than you—his name is Ved—but he has not got so many toys as this. Not at all.'

He knew he was talking with sickly falseness, but he felt ill at ease with this rich man's child and could not speak to him as he would have done to his own boy.

Haribhai stood in front of him and looked him up and down. Once.

'Garden,' he said. 'Garden. Now.'

'No, no. You cannot go to the garden just yet. Perhaps those bad men who took you in the car are still there.'

'They went away, you stupid,' said Haribhai.

Ghote felt the justice of this. There was, he thought, no real reason why Haribhai should not play outside now, with some supervision. A kidnapping is not so easy to arrange that two can be carried out in one morning. But he had his loyalty to Mr Desai. He tried changing the subject.

'Tell me about the bad men,' he said. 'What did they look like? How many of them were there?'

'The one who talked with us was nice,' said Haribhai. 'He had sweetmeats.'

'Good. And what did he look like?'

'The one driving the car had no hands,' Haribhai said.

Ghote gave up. He had not entirely agreed with Superintendent Karandikar in his sharp dismissal of the powers of observation of four-year-old boys. He would have thought his own Ved at that age might have been able to supply useful descriptive details, though it was a little difficult to pin down what he had been able to do when. However a car driver without hands was decidedly not helpful. Perhaps the superintendent was right after all. He would leave it to him to get what had to be got out of the ayah.

'Let's put this horse on his feet again,' he suggested, going over to the big, gaily-painted, dapple-grey rocking-horse.

'Stupid horse,' Haribhai said.

'Why is he stupid?' Ghote asked, beginning to get on terms with the boy.

'Stupid horse,' Haribhai repeated, evidently not on terms with Ghote. 'Stupid horse. Stupid man.'

'Why am I a stupid man?' Ghote asked, heaving the rocking-horse upright.

'Dective,' said Haribhai. 'Dectives have round things.'

In a moment he was down on hands and knees, peering through a magnifying-glass—made of air, but plain as plain to see—at some particularly juicy clue on the floor.

Ghote was impressed.

'How did you know about magnifying-glasses?' he asked, seizing an airy one himself, dropping on to all fours and inspecting the juicy clue in his turn.

'From comics, stupid,' Haribhai said.

'Of course. You are quite right. Often I have seen, when my Ved has a comic.'

69

'I have all the comics,' Haribhai stated. 'Stupid man.'

Ghote looked at the fat face so close to his own as they knelt together.

'Why am I a stupid man now?' he asked.

'Not decting,' Haribhai said.

Sadly Ghote reflected that Superintendent Karandikar had forbidden him to do any detecting. And then an idea broke open like a soft rose in his mind.

'Would you like to be a detective with me?' he asked Haribhai.

'No,' said Haribhai.

'No?'

'It is you who can dective with me.'

'All right. Well, I will tell you what we have to find. A most important clue. When the bad men tried to take you away they left a letter for your daddy.'

'That is not decting, stupid.'

'Ah, no, the letter is not. But the letter was in envelope, and often you find very good clues from envelopes. So what we have to do is to find that envelope.'

Haribhai got to his feet. He gave Ghote a look of pitying scorn. He went over to a wastepaper basket decorated with a gay line of marching red elephants. He stooped. And he held up a coarse brown envelope, lightly crumpled.

CHAPTER FIVE

Ghote took the envelope that little Haribhai was contemptuously presenting and, holding it carefully by one corner just in case at some future time there might be confirmatory fingerprints still to be lifted from it, he looked at it. There was not a lot to see. It was very much like any other envelope of its type, the sort used for the everyday purposes of commerce. It was made of the cheapest paper, coarse, dark brown in colour with small blotches of half-absorbed lighter stuff. It had been sealed and had been roughly torn open. On its front, in the same crude characters as the note it had held had been written in, there was scrawled in red MR DESAI. The only mildly remarkable thing was that, instead of being the usual oblong shape, it was completely square.

For a moment this puzzled Ghote. He felt it ought to mean something to him. But he had only a moment to brush against the thought: Haribhai was making his comment.

'What is a clue?'

Ghote took a long breath.

'A clue is something that helps you to know who has done something,' he offered cautiously.

'Like who pushed me out of that car?'

'Yes. That would be one thing.'

'Then who did?'

'We have to find that out still.'

'But you said envelope would be clue. Why are you not knowing now?'

Haribhai eyed the square brown envelope with accusation plain in his over-fat face.

'Well,' Ghote said, 'I am sorry to tell that this envelope does not seem after all to provide any clue.'

'Garden,' Haribhai commanded. '*Ek dum.*'

Argument continued for some while. Ghote was even a minute or so late sending out the second servant for Superintendent Karandikar to interview. And he was still fighting a sporadic rearguard action when the ayah returned, happily well within the superintendent's thirty-minute limit. But she looked by no means the merely harassed, leathery figure who had left. Now tear stains were easy to see on her cheeks. Her sari was over her head and its corner was visibly wet with earlier sobbings. Her lips were twitching still. There could be no doubt that down at the Rite-Wite Cleaners' shop she had endured a formidable inquisition.

But she was back. She had not been arrested. So it was almost certain that it was not she who had given away any details of the Desai household routine.

Would it be one of the other servants? Or would it after all prove to be only persistent observation that had helped the kidnappers to plan their snatch?

Ghote realized that these would be questions now to which Superintendent Karandikar alone would eventually learn the full answers. All he himself had to do was to go on organizing the flow of witnesses that might or might not provide the answers. And secretly he began to wish that somehow he might still be in charge of the whole affair.

But then he admitted a distinct relief that that terrible responsibility had been taken away from him. A life was at stake. Thank God, it was not in his hands.

*   *   *

He was to find soon enough, however, that the cup was not so easily to be passed on.

It was a little after midday and he was sharing, without much appetite, an enormous lunch that was being served to Mr Desai on the big, round, highly polished Burma teak table of the penthouse dining-room. He had sent off the last of the servants to Rite-Wite Cleaners and was wondering what, if anything, Superintendent Karandikar would find for him to do next.

The telephone rang.

'Take, take,' said Mr Desai, his mouth full of yellow-sauced chicken biryani. 'It would be for you.'

He waved sauce-drippy fingers towards a corner table and another of his boasted telephones. It too was white.

Ghote went across and answered it. Superintendent Karandikar's voice sprang out at him.

'Ghote?'

'Speaking, Superintendent. Here, Superintendent.'

'You will be glad to know, Inspector, that, thanks to your delay in getting out after witnesses to the snatch, the reports I have had have been thoroughly bad. The getaway car was seen by five separate people. It is a Ford. It is an Ambassador. It is a Chevrolet. It is a Fiat. It is a Herald.'

'I am sorr—'

'The driver had a beard. At least we have established that. According to a Sikh fortune-teller who works on the corner of the back lane, the man is a Muslim. According to a Muslim female witness, the man is undoubtedly Sikh. And the other person involved in the snatch was wearing white

74

trousers, or khaki. Either with a red check shirt, or perhaps a blue one, checked, or possibly striped. He was either 180 centimetres tall, or definitely 150. So what is to be done, Inspector?'

Ghote, schooled in the British days of feet and inches, was having to do some swift arithmetic to convert to the now mandatory metric scale—how typical of Superintendent Karandikar, he thought, to be able to use it automatically—and he took a moment or two to reply. But hardly had he begun to utter something than the Superintendent broke in.

'Nothing to be done? I thought as much, Inspector. Well, let me tell you what I am doing. I am going like hell for our only chance remaining.'

'Yes, Superintendent,' Ghote answered, pumping enthusiasm into his voice.

'And what is that? It is the white box they are leaving down on the shore for the money. They made a couple of bad mistakes in talking about that.'

'Yes, sir. A place near where the road comes down to the sea, and then the mention of rocks.'

'They spoke about rocks, Inspector. Well now, it may not have occurred to you, but that means some shore areas and not others. And there is the matter of access also.

75

Another limiting factor there, you know. I have had men working on the maps from the moment that call ended. There are plenty of possible places, of course. But if those fellows intend to keep within a reasonable distance of Cumballa Hill, then there are not so many that they cannot all be thoroughly dealt with.'

Ghote made no comment. Without maps he had been able to think during the course of the morning of too many possible places for the drop for it to be worthwhile speculating about any of them.

'Inspector, you are there?'

'Yes, Superintendent. Listening, Superintendent.'

'So you had better join one of my search parties, Inspector. There are forty of them, one is bound to need you. Searchers are divided into three groups, those dressed as dhobis, those dressed as fishermen, those dressed as scavengers. At the last count the dhobis were fewest, so get up to your home straightaway, get your wife to make up a good bundle of washing, get stripped down to an old dhoti and report to me by telephone for further instructions.'

'Yes, sir. Very good, sir.'

A small rôle, Ghote thought. One unlikely to help find little Pidku, but something that had to be done. Because Superintendent

76

Karandikar was certainly right about the possibilities of identifying the kidnappers having been reduced to making contact with them at the time they hoped to secure the ransom money. With reports from witnesses as contradictory as those he had spoken of, and with the Desai servants almost certainly not having been accomplices to the business, this was now their last chance.

Or was there one more tiny lead?

One other thing had struck him as he had thought about the affair after his spell as temporary ayah. It was something so small as hardly to exist, but should he nevertheless mention it to Superintendent Karandikar? Or would that be taken as an attempt to retain for himself the major part in the case that the superintendent so plainly thought him unfitted for?

He wanted to leave it. The notion of that tiger tongue flicking out, laceratingly, was terribly intimidating. And it was only the matter of an impression. But then it was something the superintendent could not know about. And it was quite probable that, however big the search for the waiting white box, it would fail. And then this one faint lead might be all that lay between a five-year-old boy and brutal death.

'Superindent Karandikar, sir. There is one

thing.'

'Ghote, I want to speak to Mr Desai. Now.'

'Sir, in a conversation I noted this morning I gained the impression that the sum demanded—'

'Inspector, I do not want your impressions.'

Ghote longed to stop. What he had to say concerned, there could be no getting round it, an intimate discussion between Mr and Mrs Desai, and Mr Desai was sitting there just behind him. He would by no means care to think that a mere lowly policeman had been pondering over such intimacies. And yet it might be significant.

He glanced over his shoulder. Mr Desai was fishing in a large silver bowl for a round, orangey-brown gulab jamun from the syrup in which it floated. He would hear every word. But the image of the old tailor, battered by defeat, was in Ghote's mind and would not be exorcised.

He turned back to the telephone, lowered his voice and spoke with rapidity and determination.

'Sir, I heard some talk between Mr Desai and his wife. It made me think that the sum of twenty lakhs is the very utmost that he could pay, and I am asking, 'How did the kidnappers know that?' Sir, it may be that—'

'Thank you, Inspector. And I have said I wish to talk to Mr Desai.'

'Yes, sir. Very good, Superintendent.'

Ghote turned away from the telephone. The manufacturer of Trust-X had got the fat, round gulab jamun into his mouth. He was chewing heartily and at the same time wiping the tips of his fingers on his working lips.

'Superintendent Karandikar would like to speak with you, sahib,' Ghote said.

Manibhai Desai concentratedly pushed himself up from the shining teak table and came over. He took the receiver.

'Desai.'

Ghote wondered whether to leave the penthouse there and then. He had been given his orders, after all. But nevertheless he felt he wanted to say something in parting to the manufacturer of Trust-X. Quite what it was he was uncertain of. He could not beg him to find as generous a ransom sum as possible for Pidku. Indeed, it was perhaps his duty really to back up Superintendent Karandikar in his forceful advice not to pay the kidnappers anything. And yet he wanted to say something to stiffen the rich man's once-made resolution to provide at least some money to save the boy.

If it would save him ... If kidnappers

could ever be relied on . . .

Ghote waited, trying to sort out in his mind the contrary phantoms that rose shrieking there.

'Very well, Superintendent,' he heard Mr Desai say after a while. 'I will arrange for a sum in old notes as they suggested. But I will see to it that every number is recorded in case this second-line plan of yours goes wrong.'

There was a sharp interjection.

'But Inspector Ghote seemed to think—' Mr Desai said in answer.

Again Superintendent Karandikar spluttered angrily at the far end. And then the manufacturer of Trust-X abruptly straightened himself to his full height.

'Mr Karandikar,' he said, with a coldly biting edge to his voice that Ghote had known must exist though he had yet fully to hear it. 'Mr Karandikar, you will allow me to make my own judgments.'

A swift interposed splutter. And then the manufacturer of Trust-X spoke again at his coldest and most decisive.

'Superintendent, I insist to have Inspector Ghote by me here until this whole business is cleared up. Do I have to ring the Commissioner to get my way?'

A different-sounding voice at the far end. After it had finished Mr Desai said briefly,

'Then we will carry on from here, goodbye.' And then he replaced the white receiver with a distinct flourish of triumph.

'Inspector Ghote,' he added, 'your Superintendent Karandikar requests me to say that he has changed your orders. You are to stay here and act as my contact with your colleagues in all things so long as I wish. I shall be relying upon your advice.'

He gave Ghote a long, penetrating look from his deep-set eyes. Ghote felt the judgment proceeding. Would the advice he would be asked for prove correct? What an intolerably weighty affair he was being asked to consider.

The responsibility settled across his shoulders like leaden sacks at the end of his yoke.

And it was immediately brought into play.

'Superintendent Karandikar intends in the event of the search for the white box not being successful that I should keep the rendezvous those men give,' Mr Desai said. 'He tells me he will provide a quantity of paper to look like the ransom sum, but asks that I should supply some real notes also. I tell you I do not altogether rely on even this plan working. So how much money should I offer so that if these men get away with their white box they would be appeased?'

81

Ghote's first thought at what he heard was to rejoice; the mute appeal that the tailor had made at the start of the day was still having its effect. Mr Desai was prepared to risk some considerable sum to save Pidku. Then came anxiety, gnawing like a rat. What if in fact Superintendent Karandikar's second-line plan should go wrong, as Mr Desai had thought it might? What if the kidnappers, who must be prepared to find an attempt was being made to catch them as they lifted the ransom, did get away with the white box and found in it not the twenty lakhs they expected but some smaller sum? Would they at once decide to issue their dreadful warning to any future victims? The warning that would take the form of five-year-old Pidku's rejected body?

But if he advised the proprietor of Trust-X to substitute for Superintendent Karandikar's paper a really large sum of money and if that sum was somehow spirited away, what personal retribution would await him then? And it might not only come from the superintendent. It might come from Mr Desai as well, Mr Desai with the Commisssioner's ear, feeling suddenly that he had been over-persuaded into parting with a sum that his young and loved wife would disapprove of.

And even if the kidnappers were given every anna they asked, they might still simply present a new demand.

The thoughts rose up, struck their lances, disappeared, streaming this way, streaming that.

Manibhai Desai awaited his answer.

'It would not be right for me to tell,' Ghote said at last. 'Truly there are good arguments for every course. We know nothing of these men: we cannot say what would be for the best.'

'Then what shall I do?' Mr Desai asked.

His deep eyes looked luminous with a hunger.

'You must do as the heart says,' Ghote replied, finding the words came.

For almost a whole silent minute the manufacturer of Trust-X stood where he was.

Was he consulting his heart, Ghote wondered. It looked as if he was. But what heart was there to consult?

The door of the dining-room opened quietly and a bare-footed bearer entered. Immediate and brilliant anger flashed up into Manibhai Desai's eyes.

'Get out, get out, get out,' he yelled.

The door shut more noisily than it had opened. Mr Desai strode like a whirlwind across to the telephone, seized the receiver and dialled a number. Ghote saw that the finger that sought the dialling holes trembled.

The phone was answered.

'It is Mr Desai. Put me through to Mr Shah. At once.'

A voice, flustered to pieces it was easy to tell, asked a question.

'To Mr Shah, Head of Accounts, you fool. What other Mr Shah is there? Do you know nothing?'

Ghote waited. Plainly the proprietor of Trust-X had made his decision. What sum would he ask to be gathered together now in old notes of fifty and one hundred rupees value? How many would he order to have their numbers carefully listed, to be bundled neatly together, to be brought up in haste to the penthouse on Cumballa Hill ready to be taken, if necessary, to the rendezvous when he was given it at six o'clock? Just what sum would he pay for Pidku, the tailor's son?

CHAPTER SIX

The delay at the far end of the telephone line, at what Ghote realized must be the factory of Trust-X Manufacturing (Private) Ltd., extended nerve-stretchingly. Manibhai Desai fumed. Every three or four seconds he would begin some fierce command to whoever was on the other end, and then he would fretfully abandon it. Ghote felt himself almost as tense.

'Shah? Is that you, Shah?'

Mr Desai's words smacked out at last like a volley of gunshots.

'Now listen to me. I need a large sum of money in old notes. In old fifty- and hundred-rupee notes, and I need it quickly. You will go to the bank yourself and—'

A voice at the far end said something.

'You will not talk when I am talking,' Manibhai Desai said.

The words sent an ice-dagger of despair into Ghote. He could hardly imagine anything more abrupt and overbearing being said to a man who after all must rank as a senior executive at Trust-X Manufacturing. Would the person capable of uttering such words ever spend as much as ten rupees only on helping someone like the old tailor?

'You will go to the bank yourself,' Mr Desai resumed harshly. 'Anything else can be done afterwards. And you will take away on my instructions in old notes the sum of one lakh. One lakh.'

Ghote hardly heard Mr Desai's abrupt and precise directions about having the numbers of the notes recorded, about having them bundled up and about how they should be brought up to the penthouse by Mr Shah in person. Instead he stood and marvelled at the size of the sum that Mr Desai had decided on.

It was, of course, only one twentieth of that demanded. But it was nevertheless in itself a very considerable amount, equal to his own skimpy pay for as much as twenty years to come.

And surely it would be enough for these men? The one who had talked on the telephone, who was likely to be the leader, was beyond doubt a rough individual. Such a man would find a whole lakh of rupees a fortune. Surely they would settle for it? And if their wilder hopes had been dashed, would they not still calculate that to release little Pidku in exchange for this comparatively moderate sum would serve only to improve any future market they might try?

Yet difficulties without number still lay

ahead. Superintendent Karandikar's searchers might yet come across the white box and the superintendent mount a huge, military-scale, extra-efficient ambush during which the kidnappers might kill Pidku at the very moment they were arrested. Or, if the box were not found, the same thing might occur when the manufacturer of Trust-X kept the kidnappers' rendezvous. And there was the whole question behind that of how much trust it was ever possible to put in such men.

But in any case there was nothing to do now but wait. Wait for how long? And, if he was going to have to stay in the penthouse till perhaps a very late hour of night, then one thing he would have to do would be to telephone his wife.

She would not like his news. He had been busy with purely routine work before the moment of that fateful meeting with the Commissioner by the steps of Headquarters, and he had thus felt it safe to allow Protima to believe that on this occasion he would certainly come home at the end of office hours.

Nor did he much care for intruding his private affairs on the proprietor of Trust-X by asking to use his telephone. But he would have to do so. After all, he owed things to his wife.

And now was the time. Manibhai Desai had barked his last instructions to the unfortunate Mr Shah and had put down the telephone receiver.

'Please,' Ghote said. 'I would be very grateful to ring up my wife. By six o'clock when we are hearing from that fellow again she will expect me at home.'

'Use, use,' Mr Desai said, gesturing expansively at the telephone.

He turned away and his eye caught the still cluttered lunch table.

'Why cannot anybody in this house do anything when they should?' he shouted in fury.

While he was yelling for the bearer, whom he had so unceremoniously ejected not long before, Ghote hastily dialled his home number.

He had to wait a little for the phone to be answered, and felt a growing impatience. To keep this friend of the Commissioner hanging about while he held a private conversation was not right.

But at last Protima answered. Ghote took a quick breath and stated the facts as briefly as he could, carefully refraining from saying who it was who had been made the victim of this kidnapping at second hand. If details of the affair got to the Press sooner than Superintendent Karandikar had bargained for, then he wanted to be sure there was no possibility of blame being attached to him.

Protima seemed to receive the blow of his late return well.

'Then you will come back perhaps late tonight, perhaps even tomorrow?' she asked.

'Yes, yes, I am afraid it will be that. But I must ring off now. So take care of yourself, and tell little Ved to be a good boy.'

He had a momentary vision of his son, coupled with the thought of what it might feel like if for some inexplicable reason he should be kidnapped.

'Lock the door of the house,' he said hastily to Protima. 'You know I have my key.'

'There is no need.'

Her voice was suddenly tense and harsh. Ghote shot out a question before he could help himself.

'No need? No need? Why is there no need? Listen, there are men who—'

'I shall not sleep if you are not here.'

That cold statement. And it was not really even true. Many a time he had come back late after she had made such a threat only to find her asleep and peacefully so. But the threat always had power to disturb him. It was

Protima's weakness to have periods of sleeping badly, and he worried about them. And she knew it.

'But, yes,' he said, 'you must sleep, or tomorrow you will be tired all day.'

And then he suddenly wanted to ask her if she had taken that day's Trust-X tablet. There were times when she forgot, and when she did she perhaps seemed more irritable the following day. So a missed Trust-X combined with a night of no sleep would be a bad combination.

But somehow with the proprietor of Trust-X standing just behind him, calmly and unashamedly listening, he felt he could not mention the product. Hastily he paraded in his mind some alternative ways of asking. 'Have you taken the thing from the white envelope?' '. . . the thing that comes monthly?' No, no, no.

'Well,' he said, trying to get some cheerfulness into his voice and knowing he was going to fail. 'Well, do your best. And I will see you when I will see you. Goodbye.'

He waited a little to see whether Protima would say goodbye to him. If she did, it would mean she was secretly acknowledging that the quarrel was over. She said nothing. He put down the receiver.

The afternoon was terrible. Time crawled. There was virtually nothing that had to be done. Manibhai Desai sent his cheque for one lakh to his bank and Ghote took advantage of the messenger to send the kidnappers' note and its envelope to the forensic laboratories. But after that the proprietor of Trust-X refused to take any decisions till it was certain Superintendent Karandikar's massive search of the rocky parts of the Bombay shoreline had failed. But as the hours went by Ghote began to have more and more doubts about what success could come of searching six miles — ten kilometres, Superintendent Karandikar would have said — of wide shoreline.

It was even quite possible that the kidnappers had been keeping watch on the white box and had been alerted by the presence further along the shore of dozens of dhobis making no attempt to do any clothes-washing. They could then have spirited the box away before the searchers got to it and have even put it back after the dhobis, or the boatless fishermen, or the unusually methodical scavengers, had passed by.

But speculation about what was going on was pointless.

Which did not stop the manufacturer of Trust-X from frequently indulging in it, and from regularly insisting that Ghote get in touch with Superintendent Karandikar and ask what progress had been made. Ghote fought off these requests as well as he could, but more than once he had to succumb. And, when he did so, the fact that Superintendent Karandikar knew perfectly well that the inquiry was being made at the behest of Manibhai Desai did not stop him rasping the inquirer as if his tongue was indeed the harsh tongue of the tiger.

Ghote, to some extent, had his own back on the proprietor of Trust-X by suggesting after each call that they ought to tell the father of the missing boy there had been no progress, for there never was anything more hopeful to say.

The first time Manibhai jibbed horribly.

'But, no,' he said.

'But he would want to know.'

'But there is nothing to tell.'

'Even that would be something. He can believe that we in the police are doing our utmost.'

'I am not sure if that is really the case.'

'But, nevertheless, sahib, do you not consider that you should say something?'

And then a sudden flush of fury on those

bold features.

'If you are so insisting the man should be told, then do the telling yourself.'

Ghote went and told the poor tailor his non-news, and did so again each time he made inquiries.

At four o'clock Mrs Desai came back from the Beat Contest in aid of the Bihar Flood Victims. She did recount the success of the contest and tell with enthusiasm of the large sum that had been raised to help the distant sufferers from disaster.

And, although at first Ghote had reacted with secretly shocked disapproval, the very liveliness she brought to her account of the different sums that had been raised in various ways and of the prizes that had been won by this group or that penetrated bit by bit after a while the armour he had buckled on against her.

Her cherry-red fingernails danced as she described the way the winning group played. They danced again and her eyes shone as she demonstrated the size of the big head-thrust-upwards pottery horse that had been the first prize in the tombola. It was easy to join in with her enthusiasm. Her husband did so with a smile on his wide mouth for the first time that day. And, no doubt, the Commissioner's wife, had she been there, would have delighted in this lively, kameez-clad, modern and gay figure as if she were indeed her own daughter.

And, after all, Ghote thought with a perceptible relaxation of the taut muscles of his back, life must go on. The dark problem that had occupied his day like a massive, over-hanging monsoon cloud was only one problem. Life, to get anything ever done, had to be bigger than any one of its problems.

Then, in the immediate aftermath of all the gaiety just when Mrs Desai had left them to go and get changed, Mr Shah arrived.

When the door bell rang Ghote himself opened it on Manibhai Desai's instructions, though he declined to produce the Enfield .380. That he had contrived, as long ago as when he had volunteered for his stint as deputy ayah, to put into a drawer in the front of the mock-rosewood telephone table.

Mr Shah, standing at the threshold, cast an instant gloom on the bubble jauntiness that had irradiated the penthouse with Mrs Desai's return. He was a lean individual of about forty, he was dressed in a greying white suit so extraordinarily frayed at the cuffs and so greasily worn at the collar that the eye kept returning to it despite every better resolution. It was only with a distinct effort indeed that it was possible to take in the face, anyhow largely concealed by a big pair of dulled and battered-looking horn-rim spectacles. And then there did not seem to be anything much more to see than a drawn and worried pattern of lean flesh.

But there was one other strongly notable thing about Mr Shah: chained to his right wrist he carried a Gladstone bag of stout leather.

It was this that immediately claimed Mr Desai's attention. He took one look at the accountant and spoke in a fierce, subdued mutter.

'Quick, you fool,' he said, 'come in at once and go through to the—'

But at just that moment Mrs Desai, all gaiety and lightness and smooth living still, came back into the hall.

The proprietor of Trust-X turned swiftly away from Mr Shah and attempted to say something to her. But it was plain that he could not at all think of anything to say. And in the meantime Mr Shah, with quick and almost slinking obedience, did as he had been asked and came scuttling into the luxurious, Mizrapur-carpeted hall.

'I am sorry if I am late,' he said, in the rapid patter of excuse. 'It took a great deal of time to record all the numbers of the notes.'

'Notes?' said Mrs Desai, at once all

95

sharpness and alertness. 'What notes are these?'

And then her eyes took in the heavy leather bag chained to Mr Shah's wrist.

She whirled on her husband.

'You are going to pay for that boy,' she accused him. 'You have gone against every word I have said. You are going to pay. How much?'

But Manibhai Desai was prepared to fight.

'Yes,' he retorted, spreading out his broad shoulders like a defensive wall. 'I am going to pay for that boy. It is the least I can do.'

'How much? How much? How much?'

Ghote, transfixed beside the depressing Mr Shah as an unwilling spectator to the scene, saw that with each repeated question Mrs Desai stamped a narrow, long, petulant foot.

'What I spend is my own affair,' her husband answered her loftily.

'It is your affair, is it? To spend money that can be used to buy the things I need, that I want. That is your affair only?'

'When have I ever denied, when ever?' Mr Desai shouted back, apparently feeling on safer ground now.

'I am asking: how much for that boy?' his wife countered, skilfully falling back to her strongest position.

'I am not telling.'

Mrs Desai, cherry-red nails held talon-wise, swung away from him. She brought all her forces abruptly to bear on the grey Mr Shah.

'How much have you brought?' she demanded.

Her husband equally swung to face the accountant.

'You are not to tell,' he thundered.

'You will tell me,' Mrs Desai said, a fury of command in her voice.

'It is not much,' Mr Shah said, placatingly.

But his words did nothing to stem the darting anger in Mrs Desai's whole face. Mr Shah swallowed.

'It is about half a lakh only,' he said.

'Fool.'

Manibhai Desai flung out the word. Mr Shah retreated a step and tried to raise his right arm in self-defence perhaps against an expected slap. The weight of the heavy leather Gladstone bag was too much for him.

But, luckily, his employer's attention was soon enough diverted.

'Fool, is it?' Mrs Desai screamed. 'It is you who are the fool, Manibhai. Half a lakh? You would give half a lakh for that tailor's brat?'

'He is the only son,' Mr Desai replied, actually cringing a little now.

'I do not care if there are twenty sons,' Mrs

97

Desai flung back. 'You would give half a lakh? When we would soon be needing new car. When both cars we would soon be needing to replace, and you are well knowing what must be paid to get to the top of the list. Fool. Fool. And fool again.'

Ghote, beside the gradually relaxing Mr Shah, wondered if with this assault he would not see the strongminded manufacturer of Trust-X actually reduced to grovelling. But he was in for a surprise.

Manibhai Desai's bold-featured face was only for a few instants a picture of retreat. Soon enough an expression of calm resolution unexpectedly emerged.

'Perhaps fool it is,' he said, with a new quietness. 'But at some time a man must be a fool for the sake of God.'

Mrs Desai was unimpressed.

'God? God?' she said. 'When were you ever at a temple? When? When? Never, except at Diwali when you make offerings you do not believe because they are in honour of Lakshmi. Yes, the goddess of riches will make even you half-believe.'

'I may not go to temples,' Manibhai Desai replied. 'And, very well, perhaps I do not believe in God. I do not know. But I know this. There comes at last a time for giving.'

'But giving you are always and plenty,' his

98

wife answered, countering this new, quieter tone with a calm reasoning voice of her own. 'Trust-X Manufacturing is often leading the list of givers. Look at today. None gave a prize half as good at Trust-X. And that was in aid of flood victims. What better, if you must be giving?'

'That is not the same thing,' her husband answered, his deep-set eyes suddenly sparkling in a new fury.

'Not the same? To give is to give. Come now, Mani, stop this foolishness. It is well to give, if you want. But all things must be done with common sense only.'

She put a hand, long-fingered, cherry-nailed and pleading, on to his arm. He made no attempt to throw it off.

Ghote abruptly and sharply feared for little Pidku.

'Besides,' Mrs Desai went on wheedlingly, 'are the police doing nothing? In taxes how much do we pay? Surely they must be doing something?'

And, to Ghote's plummeting dismay, she swung round to him, inquiry written plainly on her bird-like, beautifully made-up features. She should not have even realized in the midst of such a dispute that he was here at all: it was starkly unfair.

He cleared his throat.

'The case is under the care of Super-intendent Karandikar,' he said. 'He is an officer universally respected for his great effic-iency.'

'And he is doing what?' Mrs Desai demanded, as if a Superintendent Kar-andikar could be like a servant or shop-man, all promises and no performance.

'At this moment,' Ghote replied with some dignity, 'perhaps the most massive search of the Bombay shoreline ever to be carried out is in progress. The criminals were unwary enough to betray to us that they have left a white box to receive the ransom sum placed between two rocks somewhere on the shore. As of now some hundreds of police, under the disguise of dhobis, fishermen and scavengers also, are fine-tooth combing the whole area so that when that box is found a full-scale ambush may be mounted.'

'And if they do not find?' Mrs Desai said sharply.

'In that eventuality,' Ghote answered, 'Superintendent Karandikar has already set up a fail-safe plan.'

A snicker of pleasure went through him as he hit on the expression 'fail-safe'. That if anything should convince Mrs Desai of the CID's up-to-date efficiency.

'And what is this fail-safe plan?'

'A fail-safe plan is a plan—'

'Do you think I am not knowing what is fail-safe? Do you think I am reading nothing? No magazines? Nothing? What is the plan itself I am asking?'

Ghote offered a slight apologetic cough.

'In the event of a failure to locate the ransom drop site,' he said, 'the super-intendent would request your husband to keep the rendezvous offered by these criminal elements, and he would arrange for your husband to be followed so that the men can be seized at the moment of the handover.'

'My husband to be followed,' said Mrs Desai, still not impressed enough. 'And if these men see you policemen following, what then? They will seize the money and make their escape.'

Here Manibhai Desai interrupted quickly.

'But Superintendent Karandikar is to supply false money,' he said.

'False money?'

Mrs Desai swung back round to him, and Ghote knew that at that moment he himself had once again ceased to exist for her.

'False money?' Mrs Desai repeated, all concentration on her husband. 'Then why are you having brought here that?'

She flicked five cherry-red fingernails in a gesture of pure disdain out towards Mr Shah,

101

or towards the Gladstone bag.

Manibhai Desai bit his underlip.

'I have ordered that money,' he said, gathering resolution, 'because in the event of the kidnappers getting away with the supposed ransom I wish to give them at least such a sum as will induce them after all to surrender the little boy, Pidku.'

'But already I am saying that you give and give plenty. Why give so much for this one boy only?'

A small frown came on to the high, sloping forehead of the proprietor of Trust-X. It came there and stayed.

'Somehow,' he said, 'I am feeling it is not the same thing to give for others as to give for him.'

Ghote would have liked to join in the discussion here. He would have liked to step forward and produce the answer to the conundrum disturbing Mr Desai. Only he knew that he and Mr Shah had now more than ever to efface themselves. And besides he could not produce the conundrum's answer.

But he saw that Mrs Desai was looking with calculation at the puzzledly obstinate expression on her husband's face, and in a moment she spoke on a new note.

'Perhaps giving to many is the same,

perhaps it is not,' she said with a sudden lightness. 'But in any case let us not worry about it just now.'

She turned briefly to Mr Shah.

'You can take the cash back to office now,' she said quickly. 'See that it is put in the safe, and get it to the bank again first thing tomorrow.'

Mr Shah gave a half smile of acknowledgment and began slowly to sidle towards the wide front door.

'Stop,' said the proprietor of Trust-X. 'Stop. There is a difference.'

Mr Shah stopped, but cast an inquiring glance at Mrs Desai. She was beginning a brusque gesture to order him out when her husband resumed.

'No, there is a difference,' he said. 'I will tell you what it is. I know it here.'

His large and expansive hand, that not so long before had been on the point of landing—slap—on Mr Shah's hornrim-protected face, smote himself somewhere in the region of his large hand-printed silk necktie.

'I know it here,' he repeated. 'It is the tailor. That is the difference between the two sorts of giving: the tailor is here. In this house. In this flat. It is because he is here that I must pay for his son.'

103

'But he is not our servant at all,' Mrs Desai argued frowningly.

'It is not that, it is not that,' her husband said, shaking her claims off like a persistent fly. 'It is that I have spoken to the father. He and I have spoken face to face. I must pay. I will pay.'

And the argument was evidently finally decided, though Ghote noted with an inner disquiet that Mr Desai ordered his accountant into the dining-room to hand over the money with the evident purpose of concealing from his wife that the Gladstone bag contained not fifty thousand rupees but a whole lakh.

He would have liked the victory to have been totally sweeping. In the half-lie, he sensed, there lay the possibility of a retreat. And it might be a retreat which even in his moment of triumph the proprietor of Trust-X would be secretly pleased to have left open for himself.

CHAPTER SEVEN

The third telephone call came, once again exactly to time, at 6 p.m. precisely. Ghote and Manibhai Desai were alone in the drawing-room of the flat, the largest room of all the big, airy rooms in the penthouse, furnished with huge, soft sofas and chairs covered in bright blue raw silk, its picture windows that faced the dark blue of the Arabian Sea shaded now by striped Venetian blinds against the declining rays of the sun as they poured in from the west out of an almost cloudless sky. Some quarter of an hour earlier Mr Desai, after casting a stealthy look at one of the two gold sunburst clocks that presided over the big room and giving Ghote a surreptitious wink, had insistently reminded his wife that she had not yet changed for the evening. A little to Ghote's surprise, Mrs Desai had failed to notice this transparent manoeuvre and had left them alone with the telephone and in taut expectation of being given the kidnappers' final rendezvous.

But, in fact, when the telephone, another white one, on the handsome simulated-wood refrigerator in one corner of the big room with its somewhat oppressive blue roses

wallpaper—'England-imported', the manufacturer of Trust-X had not failed to tell
Ghote—rang, both of them had started in
surprise as if some strident fire-alarm had
pealed out into a quiet hour.

Manibhai Desai had actually spilt some
whisky—Ghote, conscious of duty, had
declined the offered drink—on to the
spongily thick red carpet and had set down
his glass on one of the many small glass-
topped tables with a clink of extraordinary
loudness. He had then rushed over to the
telephone, picked up the receiver and barked
a hoarse 'Hello' into it. But at once he had
realized that the big radiogram, on which he
had been playing to an unresponsive Ghote a
loud selection of Nat King Cole hits, was still
going at full blast.

He now signalled wildly to Ghote, who was
padding across to listen in to the conversation, to go back and switch the machine
off.

Ghote turned and ran over to the glossy
radiogram. He looked at its array of white
knobs. They were labelled bewilderingly
with such terms as 'Woofer' and 'Tweeter',
'Treble' and 'Bass'. But there did not seem to
be a single one marked simply 'On/Off'. The
noise from the long loudspeaker directly in
front of his knees was deafening. Away in the

distance, it seemed, Manibhai Desai was shouting 'Hello, hello' and 'Wait one moment only.'

They would miss the call altogether if he could not stop this cataract of sound. He felt suddenly clammy with sweat.

Then he reached forward, seized the arm above the slowly revolving record and lifted it. In the stark silence that broke in on them Manibhai Desai's shouting voice trailed rapidly away to nothing. Ghote dabbed down the fragile plastic arm somewhere, anywhere, registered a fleeting fear that he had ruined it for ever, and turned and darted across the big room again towards the telephone.

As he neared it he could hear that indelibly remembered flat voice speaking at the far end.

On the wall in front of him a big, brightly painted mask, no doubt a tombola prize won once by Mrs Desai at some such function as that morning's Beat Contest, glared down with a wide and mocking grin on its hollow mouth.

'. . . again, have you got the money?'

'Yes. Yes, I have the money,' Manibhai Desai replied, most convincingly, to the voice that Ghote had half-heard.

'Good. Then on the road I would tell you about there is one point only where there are no houses and you can get straight down to the sea. That is the place.'

'Yes, yes, I understand, no houses,' Manibhai Desai said. 'But what road is that?'

'You would find the box on the tide line,' the flat voice cut in, ignoring Mr Desai's question. 'Walk in a straight line to the sea, that will bring you to the spot. Look for a flat rock about in the shape of a gecko, but with no tail. You understand? A head and front legs and body of a gecko with the mouth open to take a fly, but no tail?'

'Yes, yes, a gecko, I understand that,' Mr Desai said, and then, realizing he had missed an opportunity to prolong a little more this hopefully traceable call, he added: 'No. Wait. I do not understand. Say it all again.'

'Like a gecko. A gecko. Bring flashlight, you would see.'

Ghote detected considerable tension in the flat voice now, this was the trickiest bit, trickiest for the kidnappers, trickiest for anyone attempting to outwit them.

'But what if I do not find?' Manibhai Desai answered, a convincing wail in his voice.

'Find. You have to. Or you are killing the boy. Find the gecko rock and look between it and the one beside. The white box is there. But it is covered in weed.'

'But even if I can find, where exactly on

108

the shore is this? You have not said.'

'Come alone,' the flat voice broke in. 'Drive to the place where the road comes to the shore, and then walk. We would be watching, and if you are not alone expect before long to see the boy's body.'

'Listen,' Manibhai Desai said urgently. 'Listen, I cannot drive. My chauffeur must come in the car. And also why cannot he come with me to the shore? It would be dark. It is a lot of money. Someone might attack me.'

Ghote held his breath. This was a critical point for Superintendent Karandikar's plan.

In a long telephone conversation the superintendent had had with Mr Desai about an hour earlier, when it had begun to look certain that the assorted searchers along the shoreline were not going to succeed—no wonder they had not, Ghote thought, with the white box so carefully hidden—they had been told that somehow they should obtain the consent of the criminals for more than one person to go to the rendezvous. The extra person was to be Ghote himself. The superintendent and Mr Desai had decided that it would be best for him to be disguised as the chauffeur and had agreed to take the risk of saying to the kidnapper on the telephone that Manibhai Desai could not drive, a minor lie it was probably safe to tell since it was seldom in fact that the manufacturer of Trust-X was not driven wherever he went. To have somebody in the car was vital to the superintendent's plan, as otherwise it would be extremely difficult to keep the decoy under surveillance. With Ghote acting as chauffeur, a walkie-talkie radio could be installed on the floor beside him and following vehicles at a safely discreet distance could be kept in contact.

Now Manibhai Desai had tried the throw. Would it succeed?

'No,' said the flat voice, after a considerable pause for thought. 'No, you cannot have anyone with you down on the shore. But if you must be driven, then bring chauffeur. But he is not to leave car. Understood?'

'Very well, very well, if you say. But where am I to go? You still have not told.'

Manibhai Desai again sounded convincing with this assumption of grumbling reluctance in ceding the less important part of what he had wanted to get. But, Ghote thought, no doubt success in business depended often enough on the ability to deceive, and the manufacturer of Trust-X would have to bargain for his raw materials in just the same way as any other manufacturer.

'Now listen again,' the flat voice said. 'And carefully.'

'I am listening. I am listening.'

'At exactly midnight go to Jacob Circle and—'

'But there is no shore there,' Manibhai Desai broke in.

'Listen,' the flat voice commanded.

'Yes, I am listening, but—'

'Make your chauffeur wait there in the car with the money. You go by yourself along Ripon Road and just in a lane on the left you would see a small hotel. It is called the Great Western Hotel. Go in there and wait for the telephone to ring. At midnight just. You understand? You understand?'

'Yes, but tell—'

The receiver at the far end was banged sharply down.

Was it possible to detect extreme haste, even panic, in that sudden sharp click? Perhaps it was. Certainly the period when panic was likely to occur had begun.

For both sides.

★　　★　　★

The time on Ghote's much-checked watch was 11.56 exactly. Four minutes to midnight. He had brought Manibhai Desai's Buick almost to Jacob Circle, approaching from the west along Clerk Road. There was very little traffic about. No difficulty should prevent them keeping the new appointment the kidnapper had given.

Superintendent Karandikar had checked out the Great Western Hotel with a thoroughness, as described in person to Mr Desai and an attentive Ghote, that was totally exemplary. And it had been established beyond doubt that the concern, squalid though it might be, was perfectly innocent of any complicity in the kidnapping.

Everybody in any way connected with it from the South Indian cook to the proprietor had been questioned by a whole squad of CID men. Each of its semi-permanent residents, travelling salesmen, itinerant healers, part-time agents for undefined businesses, had been interrogated. No one even coming to eat a vegetarian meal in its fly-haunted dining-room had escaped scrutiny. But, at the end of it all, it seemed that the only reason the kidnappers had selected the sleazy little place as the spot where the proprietor of Trust-X would receive his final instructions for the rendezvous was that it possessed a telephone, kept in the entrance lobby, and did not attract so much chance custom that the instrument was likely to be in use at midnight.

Yet Ghote had upsetting doubts on two counts.

First, he could not help wondering whether Superintendent Karandikar's very thoroughness would not betray the whole plan to the criminals. If they had kept any sort of watch on the hotel, they could hardly have failed to see the squad of detectives that had descended on it within fifteen minutes of their having given its name to the manufacturer of Trust-X. The subsequent mass-questioning could not but have been noticeable to even the most hurried passer-by if they knew what to look for.

And the second fear Ghote could not suppress arose out of the former. It had come to him more and more clearly that the operation they were seeking to defeat showed every sign of having been thought out with extreme care. To have three separate telephone calls gradually revealing the final point for the collection of the ransom surely showed that someone of considerable intelligence had worked out that it was most likely that, if the proprietor of Trust-X had defied instructions and called in the police, then they would eventually attempt an ambush at the money drop point. The counter-plan the kidnappers had devised seemed calculated to defeat all but the most wide-scale police action. No doubt when shortly after midnight Mr Desai took the call in the Great Western Hotel, his orders would be to go at top speed to the final rendezvous. There the kidnappers could be already waiting in perfect safety, and as soon as they had seen Mr Desai leave they could swoop on their white box and be away within seconds. It would be difficult indeed for any pursuers to get near them.

It was unlikely, of course, that the criminals' planner, however far-sighted, could have anticipated a police plan as immense as Superintendent Karandikar's. But nevertheless the existence of some sort of master-mind seemed plain. Especially in view of the exact figure of twenty lakhs that had been demanded. Had the kidnappers not been the victims of a chance-in-a-million mistake because the two boys had happened to change clothes, they would now be in possession of the real Haribhai Desai. And no doubt the Gladstone bag at this moment in the glass-screened, air-conditioned back of the car with the proprietor of Trust-X would have contained, not just one lakh and a note from Mr Desai, but every anna of the full sum of twenty lakhs, though it would have drained the manufacturer of Trust-X to the very bottom of his resources to raise it.

And if there was such an intelligent person at the head of the kidnappers, Ghote asked himself finally, would even the most massive operation be absolute proof against him?

Jacob Circle.

Ghote, from underneath the white cap with the shiny black peak that was ordinarily the wear of the Desai chauffeur, found a place to park just where Ripon Road left the Circle. He scurried out of the Buick's driving seat and went and opened the rear door for Mr Desai, striving as much as possible to keep his face towards the protective side of the car in case the kidnappers were watching from some hidden vantage point and knew the real chauffeur by sight.

'Do not forget,' he warned the manufacturer of Trust-X in an undertone, 'Superintendent Karandikar wishes you to shout out as loud as you can if there is any unexpected trouble at the hotel. He has men posted all round.'

'Yes, yes,' Mr Desai replied.

He sounded harassed and unhappy. Ghote did not blame him.

Getting quickly back into the Buick and the security of its dark interior, Ghote picked up the small round microphone of the walkie-talkie set from the floor beside the driving seat. He held it in his fist down under the dashboard and spoke into it in a low voice, slumping his head forward as if he were dozing.

'Decoy to Central. Decoy to Central. Over.'

'Central to Decoy. Speak louder. Over.'

Ghote glanced out of the car windows. There seemed to be nobody near. He brought the microphone up a little higher and raised his voice a degree.

'Decoy to Central. Mr Desai has left for the Great Western Hotel. Over.'

'Central to Decoy. Did you deliver warning as instructed?'

'Decoy to Central. Warning delivered. Over.'

He let Superintendent Karandikar's tiger tones resonate still in his mind. Yes, he had carried out that particular instruction to the letter. But what about the way he had aided and abetted the proprietor of Trust-X in his rejection of the superintendent's plan concerning the money?

It had happened at the meeting between the three of them which the superintendent had convened so that he could explain to Manibhai Desai the full extent of what he called his 'bandobast' for the ambush. The superintendent, spare, upright and iron grey of face, had looked, it had had to be admitted, a little ridiculous in the loose white clothes and heavy white turban of a servant, a disguise he had assumed in order to come to the penthouse without arousing suspicion should the kidnappers still have a watcher somewhere near Mount Greatest. And Ghote had said not a word when the proprietor of Trust-X, after hearing about all the arrangements, had let it be understood that he would add 'only a few hundreds' of real money to the cut paper that the superintendent had brought with him. Even later, when Mr Desai had substituted the bundles of notes amounting to a full lakh that the downtrodden Mr Shah had brought, again he let the change pass without comment.

Had he been right to have done that?

A stealthily moving figure caught his eye on the far side of the Circle near the Dhobi Ghat tank, just outside the light of the tall street lamps. But then the dimly-seen shape stopped, knelt, unfolded a bundled sheet and stretched out at full length. Only a pavement sleeper settling down for the night.

Had he been right? Ought he not to have supported the superintendent one hundred per cent? It was his superior officer whose

117

intentions he had allowed to be frustrated, after all. Ought he not to have told the proprietor of Trust-X straight out that the advice he had been given by the superintendent earlier was correct? That the only way to treat kidnappers was to refuse to have any dealings with them? To make it totally plain, even when it became necessary to employ a trick like the present one, that in the end it was a trick and that in no circumstances would such breakers of a fundamental law be treated with it?

He sighed.

Well, he had not been able, when it had come to it, to do that. He had sympathized too deeply with the manufacturer of Trust-X and the way in which he had found beneath his ambitious, forward-carving exterior a stifled beat of the heart that had said 'Pay'.

If only they had been able to trace that third telephone call. It had been longer than the others, with that moment of negotiation over whether Manibhai Desai should be allowed a chauffeur or not. It might have been possible to trace it. But it had been not quite long enough, and the dilemma thus had not been happily solved in advance.

But what about that chink of weakness that the kidnapper on the telephone had shown in allowing Mr Desai to use a chauffeur at all?

Did that not indicate that fundamentally the superintendent was right in his fierceness?

'Central to Decoy. Central to Decoy.'

The tiger voice penetrated his thoughts with startling aptness.

'Decoy to Central. Am receiving you. Over.'

'Central to Decoy. Desai has entered hotel.'

Ghote looked at the watch he had so carefully synchronized with the superintendent's own back at the penthouse. One minute to midnight.

Would that storm of inquiries at the hotel have alerted the kidnappers? Would they be aware that Manibhai Desai had flouted their instructions and called in the police? Would their answer be the dead body of little Pidku, discovered tomorrow morning somewhere conspicuous, such as lying on the grey stones by the Gateway of India or perhaps in front of the great honeycomb building of the Sachivalaya for every person working in the state secretariat, as well as all the visitors to the big India Life office next to it, to see?'

The life insurance office and that unpaid-for life: there would be a bitter joke indeed.

The seconds ticked past. On the walkie-talkie Ghote was able to hear Superintendent Karandikar checking round some of the

119

vehicles taking part in his bandobast. There were no fewer than forty-seven of them all told, private cars begged or borrowed from all over the place, commercial vans pressed into service, a few police trucks rapidly disguised with a quick coat of colour wash. Not all of them were linked to the same network as the Buick, but enough were for Ghote to get a good idea of the extent and efficiency of the bandobast.

'Central to Car 8. Central to Car 8. Car 9 reports it is able to see you. You are not on station. Increase speed by five kilometres per hour.'

And then less than a minute later.

'Central to Car 7. Central to Car 7. Car 8 reports you are visible to him. Increase speed by five kilometres per hour.'

The vehicles were patrolling on fixed routes round and round the main thoroughfares of Bombay at this midnight hour. Ghote found himself harbouring a disloyal thought that this increase in traffic at a time normally very quiet might in itself be enough to alert the kidnappers wherever they were. But he suppressed it. After all Superintendent Karandikar was efficient. Everybody acknowledged that.

'Central to Decoy. Central to Decoy. Come in Decoy.'

He snatched up the little round microphone.

'Decoy to Central. I am receiving you. Over.'

'Central to Decoy. Desai has now left hotel. Repeat Desai has now left—'

At the car door the figure of Manibhai Desai himself suddenly loomed up out of the patches of light and shadow. The men with a walkie-talkie at some vantage point looking out over the Great Western Hotel must not have been very quick passing on their message. Ghote dropped his microphone and hurried round to open the Buick's rear door for the proprietor of Trust-X.

'Is all well, sahib?' he whispered.

Manibhai Desai's face was plainly sheened in sweat even in the cool of the night. He licked the lips of his wide mouth.

'Yes. Yes. All well. I must get in.'

Ghote, with an inclination from the waist in his unaccustomed white uniform, saw Mr Desai into his seat, softly closed the car's door and almost ran round to his own place. The moment he slumped into it he pushed aside the glass panel behind him and spoke.

'What did they say? I must report instantly.'

'Yes. Yes.'

The manufacturer of Trust-X gave a deep

puff of a sigh.

'It is Dr Annie Besant Road,' he said. 'We are to be there at ten minutes past midnight, or they will not accept payment.'

CHAPTER EIGHT

As Ghote without a moment's loss of time relayed the kidnappers' message, his mind was busy over its implications. Yes, it had been just as he had expected. Dr Annie Besant Road, part of the series of main thoroughfares running more or less north and south through Bombay beside the west or Arabian Sea shore, was something over a mile away from where they were now at Jacob Circle. It would be an easy trip. Either they could go swiftly along Haines Road, straight as an arrow and with almost no traffic on it at this post-midnight hour, and then with a sharp turn left go down Dr Annie Besant Road itself till they reached the point where it was possible to get directly down to the shore. Or, it would be as simple to take Clerk Road away from the Circle, go along between the Race Course and Willingdon Club and then at the looming bulk of the Mahalakshmi Temple—where doubtless at Diwali Manibhai Desai fulfilled his rare religious duties—swing hard right, go along past the shore by Hornby Vellard and thus come straight into Dr Annie Besant Road from the other direction.

In either case it should be nicely before 12.10 a.m. that the proprietor of Trust-X got out of the car and, lugging the heavy Gladstone bag, set off on his lone walk down to the sea, at that point almost a quarter of a mile away from the road.

'Sir, I will start at once,' he concluded his brief message to Superintendent Karandikar.

'No.'

'Sir?'

'You will delay your start for four minutes, repeat four minutes, under pretence of engine difficulties.'

'But, Superintendent sahib, I would not be able to get Mr Desai to the rendezvous by the agreed time.'

'You will not arrive to time, Inspector. You will arrive ten, repeat, ten, minutes late. I need the maximum period to deploy. Understood?'

'But, Superintendent, they have threatened—'

'Inform me in three and a half minutes that you are leaving Jacob Circle. Out.'

Ghote laid down the microphone.

Never before had he felt himself so much in two minds. One half of him wanted to slip the big Buick into gear and set off along Haines Road as fast as the car's acceleration would allow, eating up the straight stretch, saving every second, and the other half of him rose up like a triple row of armed men against any such disobeying of an order. Every command that he had received in all his years in the police and had at once carried out stood like a spearman steadily holding his pointed weapon to prevent any movement in a contrary direction.

At least, Ghote thought with the rational front of his mind, I can cut the engine and begin re-starting it. But I will not necessarily stay the full three remaining minutes. I will do what I feel is right when the time comes.

Or must I do what I know is right?

His eyes were fixed, peering to redness, on the second hand of his watch as his left arm lay across the top of the Buick's steering-wheel.

'Quick, man, we must go,' Manibhai Desai said, leaning forward and speaking into the gap of the sliding glass panel between them. 'They have said ten past twelve.'

Ghote turned round.

'You did not hear?' he asked. 'Superintendent Karandikar has insisted to take an extra ten minutes. He wishes to be sure of getting his men to the point designated.'

Even as he spoke, Ghote heard from the walkie-talkie on the car floor the little metallic voices flicking out orders and acknowledgments.

'All speed to Dr Annie Besant Road, and take up station . . .'

'Ten men to take up position between . . .'

'Passing Breach Candy Baths. Over.'

Manibhai Desai did not immediately reply. But when he spoke it was with his face pressed urgently to the gap in the glass panel.

'Inspector, I think we should go now.'

The very abjectness of the tone of voice set up perversely a contrary impulse in Ghote.

'I am sorry, sahib. An order is an order.'

'But the boy. They may be ready to kill him at this moment.'

The words sent springing up in Ghote's head a vision of what might even at that instant be happening. He saw some dark corner of the shore, not far away from where the white box was hidden beside the gecko rock. Even a patch of tussocky, wind-battered grass, burnt and brown, came into his vivid mental picture, with two men crouching in its scanty shelter. One of them had a big crude watch on his wrist and was peering into the night, and the other was kneeling over the small form of Pidku, the tailor's son, one coarse rough hand pressed hard across the almost meltingly soft flesh of the boy's face, stopping the least cry, and the

126

other hand grasping a knife. Ghote saw it as a long, jagged-edged butcher's blade.

Was that happening? Was that happening now? If what the kidnappers had said was the truth, some such scene must actually be in progress.

The second hand of his own watch ticked its jerky way round the little dial.

Twenty seconds to go. Ghote started up the Buick's engine and slipped into gear, but he kept his foot on the clutch.

'Permission to go, Superintendent?' he asked into the microphone.

'In fifteen seconds, Inspector. The bandobast is proceeding according to plan.'

Ten seconds.

Ghote picked out his exact path round the Circle and into the enticing straight of Haines Road. He would be at the place in much less time than Superintendent Karandikar had counted on if there was even half the power he thought there was in the Buick's big engine.

'Central to Decoy.'

'Decoy to Central. Sir?'

'You may proceed, Inspector. But do not, repeat not, exceed twenty kilometres per hour. Over and out.'

Ghote sent the big car shooting forward. But he did not let its speedometer exceed that ordered, maddeningly stately speed.

★   ★   ★

By Ghote's watch it was the fixed-on hour of 12.10 a.m. when the sweeping headlights of the slowly advancing Buick flickered on to the high walls of the big ice-cream factory in Dr Annie Besant Road. But surely the kidnappers would give them a few extra minutes? Surely they would not carry out their terrible threat with the punctuality of a time-signal?

They were bound to give an additional five minutes, he decided.

The walkie-talkie beside him crackled into life.

'Central to Decoy. Halt where you are.'

For fifty yards, for a hundred yards Ghote continued to drive the big car at the same stately speed. But then his untaken resolution crumbled before the habit of obeying orders given.

He brought the car to a quiet halt, switched off the headlights and picked up the walkie-talkie microphone.

'Decoy to Central. Have halted, Superintendent. Do you wish Mr Desai to proceed on foot?'

If the proprietor of Trust-X set off at a run,

despite the heavy leather bag of money, perhaps he would at least get down on to the shore by 12.15 still.

'Central to Decoy. Mr Desai is to remain in the car. Repeat in the car. You will wait where you are till further orders. My dispositions are not yet completed. Over and out.'

From the glass panel behind Ghote's head came a sharp, inquiring rap. Ghote turned round.

'Superintendent Karandikar has ordered us to wait here,' he said bleakly.

'But, Inspector, already it is past 12.10,' Mr Desai said with awkward urgency. 'But perhaps they would give a little more time. If I went myself now and hurried...'

'Superintendent Karandikar has said specifically that he wishes you to remain in the car, sahib.'

'No, Inspector. That child's life is at stake. I am going.'

'Very well, Mr Desai,' Ghote answered, taking desperate pains not to let the deep satisfaction that glowed and glowed inside him show by as much as one blink in his voice. 'Very well, but I shall have to report your departure.'

'Do that, Inspector. Do that. I am not caring.'

And the proprietor of Trust-X flung open
the rear door of his big Buick and staggered
out with the heavy Gladstone bag clutched
firmly in his right hand. Ghote watched him
trot forwards in the pale gleam of the
sidelights for five or ten yards. Then he
reached for the microphone again.

'Decoy to Central. Decoy to Central.'

'Central to Decoy. Please remain off air.
All channels are urgently required.'

Quietly Ghote succumbed to the
temptation. He sat back in the chauffeur's
comfortable seat and breathed deeply in and
out. At the far extremity of the glow of the
sidelights he was able, just for one moment
longer, to make out the dim form of the
proprietor of Trust-X with the awkward
lugging shape of the Gladstone bag beside
him. He was still going forward at a
determined trot. He would get to the shore as
soon as it was possible to do so. There was
nothing more to be done.

The night was quiet. Only from the walkie-
talkie down on the floor came the occasional
swift but subdued metallic voice reporting
'In position'. Superintendent Karandikar's
bandobast was filling out its designated form
to the last tuck.

Would Mr Desai be on time? If he were to
flash the long torch he had brought with him

just as soon as he reached the place where you could get down to the shore—

In a sudden panic Ghote scrabbled round to see if the proprietor of Trust-X had forgotten the flashlight.

But no, it had gone from where he had seen it earlier on the wide and springy back seat. And then, in what now seemed to have been an incredibly short time, came the order.

'Central to Decoy. Proceed to set-down point. Please see that Mr Desai takes flashlight. Over.'

'Decoy to Central. Instructions received. Over.'

Grinning to himself with a small, bitter wryness, Ghote drove the big Buick forward to the point where abruptly to his right the huge extent of the Arabian Sea could be seen. He halted, pushed his whole head and shoulders out of the car window and peered into the darkness of the night.

Yes, quite far away on the rocky shore he could see the beam of a torch. It looked, strong though he knew it to be, pathetically tiny from up here on the road. But it was easy to spot. The kidnappers where they were waiting were bound to have seen it. And, a merciful extra, none of Superintendent Karandikar's deployed men, though they were certain to have been aware of it too, had evidently thought fit to report it back to Central. Otherwise the wrath of the superintendent would undoubtedly have broken before this.

And surely the proprietor of Trust-X had been in time. Ghote looked at his watch. It said only a few seconds past 12.20 even now. So it would not have been very long after 12.15, not very long, that Mr Desai must have reached the beach.

Behind, the sound of a car coming up fast along the road sent a rush of sweat up on his back. He pulled his head in and jerked round.

It was one of Superintendent Karandikar's disguised patrols, he realized. Evidently the superintendent planned to have cars moving at speed up and down Dr Annie Besant Road for the whole time of the drop, ready if necessary to join in an instant pursuit.

And now, not twenty yards away along the road, he could make out the bulk of a considerable group of men hiding, if not very well, beside a wall. There was even a faint murmur of subdued voices. Certainly, if the kidnappers weren't to be caught it would not be for lack of men on the ground.

But what if the criminals realized how thickly meshed the net around them was? What if in desperation they then killed

132

Pidku?

Ghote fought to get the rational side of his brain on top. Would anybody, seeing that they were on the point of arrest, be so lacking in simple sense as to commit a murder to add to their crimes? Surely not. Surely not.

From somewhere along the shore there came, in the still of the night now that the sound of the fast patrol car had died away, a solitary, faraway shout of command, only just distinguishable from the cry of some disturbed seabird.

The whole shore must be blocked off by now. What drive Superintendent Karandikar had. It might be easy enough to work out the maximum forces that would be needed to be certain these men did not wriggle through the least gap in the net, but to make sure that all those forces were got into place, to fight the delays and the unwillingnesses and to overcome, that really took a man.

Now time seemed to be dragging when, up to a few minutes earlier with that terrible deadline rawly in his mind, it had gone breakneck. In strict obedience to the kidnappers' orders, he did not attempt to leave the car. But he leant as far out as he could and strained to see and to hear what was happening down on the beach, while every now and again he noted behind him the rapid passage of another of Superintendent Karandikar's fast-moving patrols, going in either one direction or the other.

The tiny glim of Manibhai Desai's flashlight was only intermittently visible now, blocked sometimes by his body and sometimes, Ghote guessed, disappearing when the proprietor of Trust-X stooped to examine some rock that bore a slight resemblance to the fly-snapping gecko. What if he never found the place? But he must. The kidnappers would have chosen somewhere that, once you were on the spot, would be easily recognizable. After all, they wanted the money. The twenty lakhs, as they must be thinking of it as.

From the faintly gleaming still blackness of the sea stretching far away beyond the more broken black of the shore there came, very quiet at first but steadily growing louder, the sound of a motorboat engine.

So this was how they were going to grab the ransom sum?

But Ghote's first, quick thought was swiftly altered. Abruptly the distant launch switched on a searchlight and sent the cold white beam swinging in a wild arc along the shore, silhouetting for one instant indeed the familiar tall form of the manufacturer of Trust-X with his Gladstone bag. Then as abruptly the light was extinguished and the boat's motor cut. Apparently Superintendent Karandikar had thought of everything, except how to maintain constant discipline over the crew of a picket launch far out at sea.

Ghote peered on into the now restored soft darkness of the moonless night.

Another fast patrol car whirred by behind him, its tyres zizzing on the smooth road surface, its lights momentarily illuminating the luxurious interior of the Buick.

Then he thought that Manibhai Desai's torch must now be pointing towards him. Was it? Had the proprietor of Trust-X found the gecko rock? And if the one lakh was now in the weed-hidden box, would the kidnappers, when they came to read the short note that was with it, the note composed with difficulty by the two of them hours and hours ago it seemed now, would they agree to its proposal?

'*One lakh is a great sum, even for me. I pay it willingly in return for the life of the son of a man who is little to me. But I cannot ruin myself and my family. Please think of the boy's father who has no other children. Set him free.*'

And then the clear, bold signature 'Manibhai H. Desai'. Ghote, with a feeling of faint shock, had recognized it as familiar. And then he had remembered. Each card of

Trust-X tablets bore it, in personal guarantee of their efficacy.

Yes, there could be no doubt about it now: Manibhai Desai was coming back up towards the road. Were the kidnappers at this very moment inching forward on pressed-to-the-stones bellies to retrieve the box? And were Superintendent Karandikar's men down on the beach already wondering whether the slight movements they had spotted were signs of their quarry? And was someone—that man with the long butcher's knife?—still holding a horny hand across the soft mouth of the little tailor's son, ready to break in one instant that long-built, surrounding wall of respect for human life the moment he suspected betrayal?

From down on the beach just below an uncertain call came from the proprietor of Trust-X. Ghote switched on the big car's headlights.

A little over a minute later Manibhai Desai came up on to the road.

'Is it all right?' Ghote asked in a hiss of anxiety.

'I have left it,' Mr Desai replied.

*   *   *

There had been nothing more to say. Ghote

136

had realized that Manibhai Desai did not wish to talk. Would he, when they arrived back at Mount Greatest, confess and confide everything to his wife? Was she, in the privacy of the bedroom, a person different enough from the one he himself had seen for this to be possible?

So the pair of them drove along to Cumballa Hill in silence. Ghote had briefly reported on the walkie-talkie that the drop had taken place and had received a brief acknowledgment, and after that not a word was spoken in the big Buick.

Even when they got back to the penthouse they still hardly exchanged a word. Manibhai Desai asked Ghote if he would be so good as to stay for the night and arranged for a sleepy servant to bring him a rug in the huge, luxurious drawing-room. And there not much later Ghote settled down to sleep for the first time in his life on cushions of raw silk.

'Superintendent Karandikar will ring the moment there is any news.'

That had been his muzzily-spoken parting assurance to the manufacturer of Trust-X. But the telephone had remained silent.

No news. No news. The thought, for all the anxiety it generated, lulled him to sleep.

He woke with a terrible start. The white telephone over on the simulated-wood refrigerator was shrilling. The time, when he blearily contrived to see the face of his watch, was ten minutes past six.

He staggered over to the telephone and picked up the receiver, managing only to mutter an incoherent 'Hello'.

'Inspector Ghote?'

It was Superintendent Karandikar, alert as the spreading day itself.

'Yes, Superintendent. Here, Superintendent.'

'You will inform Mr Desai that at 6 a.m. precisely I gave orders for the box down on the shore to be examined. It appeared to contain exactly what Mr Desai put into it just after midnight.'

'I see, Superintendent,' Ghote said.

The sense of anticlimax descended on him like a white flood. But it was broken here and there already with black dashes of fear for little Pidku's life.

He licked his lips.

'Superintendent,' he asked, 'have you got the men?'

'If I see fit to inform you of other developments, Inspector, I shall so inform

138

you.'

'But, Superintendent, Mr Desai is bound to ask me.'

'Mm. Very well, you can let Mr Desai know that there was no sign of them at all down on the beach. No sign at all.'

'Yes, I see, Superintendent.'

'And you can tell Mr Desai also that my men on the beach have just informed me that the white box contained the sum of one lakh of rupees together with a note from Mr Desai himself. His actions were in direct contradiction to the advice I gave him, in the strongest terms. You will therefore tell him that the necessary confidence between us has ceased to exist.'

'Yes, Superintendent. Very good, Superintendent.'

'And, Inspector, I hope you were entirely ignorant of this deplorable state of affairs.'

'Yes, sir,' Ghote answered with terse blankness.

'And what does that "Yes, sir" mean, Inspector? Were you ignorant of the note and that ridiculously large sum of money? Were you, man? Yes or no?'

Ghote told the bare-faced lie. It was an affirmation of his belief that, despite all the arguments on the superintendent's side, it was right to have hoped that the kidnappers would have released Pidku for a sum of sufficient size.

The superintendent barked once and rang off.

Ghote went and prowled round the penthouse. Various servants were to be seen carrying out their early morning tasks. But of Mr and Mrs Desai there was as yet no sign. Only fat and commanding little Haribhai came marching ahead of his ayah on his way down to the garden.

Ghote was pleased to note that behind the black-skinned and leathery ayah there walked the chauffeur whose uniform he had worn the night before. At least Haribhai should be safe from a second attempt at a snatch.

It was not until a few minutes before seven that Ghote encountered the newly-risen proprietor of Trust-X in the hall. He at once told him the news, or lack of it.

'So the boy?' Mr Desai asked, his deep-set eyes suddenly glaring. 'What would have happened to him?'

'There is nothing to tell,' Ghote answered, almost hopelessly. 'Perhaps it was after all that the kidnappers were unable for some reason to go to the shore last night and that is why the money was still there.'

'It was all those police,' Mr Desai replied with iron scorn. 'At the time I thought it.

Everywhere I looked on the way to the shore there were police. In cars. Hiding by walls, and not hiding well. Out at sea there was a launch also, with a searchlight. And shouting of orders I heard down on the beach.'

'Yes,' Ghote was constrained to agree. 'It might well have been that the extent of the ambush frightened them off.'

'And now? And now?' Mr Desai asked with spearing bitterness.

He did not wait for an answer. Indeed there was no need to. The 'And now?' said everything.

But it was at this moment that the newspaper vendor who served the flats delivered the day's papers through the letter-box in the wide front door. And with them, fluttering face up to the top of the pile of heavy newspapers, was a small, cheap-looking envelope bearing in familiar crude red-pencil lettering the words 'MR DESAI'.

CHAPTER NINE

The red scrawled capital letters on the cheap envelope stared up at Ghote like a sudden flaming sword placed on his path. He knew immediately that this was the kidnappers again.

Although this envelope was not the same shape as the other and although one set of scrawled letters might look much like another, this was beyond doubt written by the same hand that had spelt out Mr Desai's name on the note left when the snatch had taken place.

'It is them,' he shouted to the proprietor of Trust-X, who was also staring at the red lettering, apparently equally transfixed. 'Quick, the news-vendor. I must see him.'

And in an instant he was tugging at the long, flat bolts, top and bottom, of the wide teak door, and had it open and was looking out at the bare landing on the top floor of the high block.

The sliding stainless steel doors of the lift were closed and anonymous. Above them the little lights of the indicator registered 'G'. The ground floor? Surely there had not been time for the news-vendor to have got all the way down to the ground? Had they both stood so long staring at that envelope?

'The newsman,' Manibhai Desai said, coming out on to the landing. 'He is forbidden to use lift. There are stairs there for the servants.'

For the first time Ghote noticed, discreetly tucked away, a narrow doorway evidently leading to the stairs with opposite it an equally narrow door that must be the servants' entrance to the penthouse.

He ran over and started to descend the stairs as fast as his legs would operate. The stairwell was as narrow as it could be, and the steep steps were in slabby bare concrete. Getting down them at speed was by no means easy. But Ghote forced himself to go as fast almost as if he were falling, holding out first one arm, then the other and letting his palms smack against the rough cement walls till they stung.

He must catch the news-vendor. Once the man had got away from the block there was no telling where he might go. It might be next day before he was located. And by then he could have well forgotten vital details of how he had been handed that letter and asked to deliver it. It ought not to be long since he had started his descent of these precipice-giddying stairs, and he would surely have no particular reason to hurry. So it ought to be all right.

Leaping and half-falling and saving himself in the grey light of the barely lit stairwell, Ghote wished he could stop for an instant, end the smacking clatter of his feet and hands and hear whether there were other steps going down ahead of him. But he dared not abate by a quarter-second the speed of his downward tumble.

And now, from below, the light of day was at every instant increasing. Would he reach the foot of the stairs without seeing his man?

And now it was the final turn, and out, through a slit of an archway, into the concrete-paved service area at the back of the high block.

There was a water-tap by the wall and a group of servants from the flats were round it, washing out cloths. Not far away from them a boy of fifteen or so was moodily examining an ancient bicycle, upended on to its saddle. To the other side a gaggle of servants' children, naked and almost naked, played on the dusty surface like a heap of scrawny-legged puppies.

'The newsman. The newsman. Where did he go?' Ghote called out with all the force of his lungs.

And, to his delighted surprise, the

144

unpromising boy with the broken bicycle at once looked up.

'Just gone by,' he said, and he pushed out an arm, the thumb roughly pointing, in the direction of the corner of the towering block nearest to Ghote.

'Thank you,' Ghote called as he ran.

He rounded the corner, and it was all over. There not ten yards away was the news-vendor, a lean-fleshed individual with his head bare, the short, dark hair turning grey, wearing a battered-looking shirt and a pair of shorts and carrying under his arm a still substantial roll of newspapers.

'Newsman, newsman,' Ghote called.

The fellow turned, pulling a paper from his bundle as if he hoped to make a quick, occasional sale, no doubt at the expense of some regular customer elsewhere.

Ghote presented himself in front of him, still panting hard from the chase.

'You delivered a letter at the flat at the top just now?' he demanded.

The news-vendor looked at him suspiciously.

'I sell papers, I am not postman,' he said.

'But you delivered a letter this morning?' Ghote countered, trying rapidly as he could to soften his tone to one of polite interchange. 'There is nothing wrong in delivering a letter.'

'What if I did do that?' the news-vendor replied cautiously, still clearly ready to take refuge in obstinate refusal to admit anything.

'It was a letter for Mr Desai, Mr Desai who lives in the penthouse at the top of the block?' Ghote asked.

'I do not know who is who,' the newsman answered. 'It is my job to take them papers. One here, one there. Who they are I do not care. Only what they want. And that they pay.'

'But at the top,' Ghote persisted, seizing on what best he could to establish good relations with this valuable witness, 'at the top where you deliver so many papers, you know that?'

'Yes, I know.'

'And they pay always, yes?' Ghote asked, hoping and hoping that the wealthy proprietor of Trust-X did indeed pay this humble vendor of newspapers with regularity.

The man shrugged his stooping, bony shoulders.

'There I am getting paid,' he agreed.

'And as you came to the block this morning, it was to there that someone asked you to deliver a letter, a letter with the name on it in red?'

'If someone asks, who am I to say no? And

besides they gave money. How should I not do what I am paid money to do?'

'Quite right, quite right,' Ghote assured him. 'But all I am asking is what sort of a person was this who gave you money?'

'It was a person,' the newsman answered. 'People are people.'

'But you must have seen something of him. It was a man? Was he tall or short?'

'Tall? Short?' the news-vendor considered. 'I cannot tell.'

'But he paid you money. He spoke with you. Was he taller than you are yourself?'

'Perhaps. A little.'

'Good. Now, was he young or old?'

But the news-vendor lacked all Ghote's pleasure in seeing the gradual emergence of a discernible person from chaos. His lean face took on again the look of dulled obstinacy it had worn before.

'I tell you I did not look,' he said. 'The papers I carry are heavy. It is a long way from the newspaper dormitory. Already I was tired. A man came up to me and asked if, for money, I could take a letter. I asked how much. He gave, and I took the letter. And still I have more papers to deliver.'

He turned away.

Ghote hurried round and blocked his path.

'This is a police matter,' he said, more

roughly. 'I am an inspector of CID. The description of that man is needed. Now, speak up.'

But he could see at once that tougher measures were being even less successful. The news-vendor's obstinate look became one of blind panic. To be involved with the police, this was a sudden nightmare and could be ended only by wishing with every cell of the mind that it was not happening.

'I do not know. Nothing I saw. Nothing.'

The words were almost inaudible.

'What is your name?' Ghote demanded.

He got no answer at first, but by putting his face close to the fear-blotted countenance in front of him and driving the question in as if it were a pointed rod he did at last obtain the muttered syllables. And then bit by bit he got the address.

'All right, go now,' he said, satisfied with this small accumulation of knowledge and able to allow his insight into the newsman's condition to produce its proper reaction.

The newsman plodded off, frightened and defeated, his bundle of papers seeming twice the burden it had been when Ghote had first spotted him.

But then, Ghote thought, what more could you expect to get out of a man like that. It would be all such a one could do to get through the business of his own life, earning in a month perhaps no more than a hundred rupees. A hundred rupees, just one of many notes that the proprietor of Trust-X had had counted out to make up that sum one hundred times greater, that he had been willing to pay to save little Pidku. But a hundred a month would mean at best squeezing yourself and your family into a single room in a tottering chawl somewhere, perhaps even sharing that with another family. How could such a man have energy for the luxury of looking about him?

And then, when the newsman was some twenty yards away and as Ghote still stared at him, standing in the bright early morning sunshine and beginning to turn over in his mind the circumstances in which the fellow might have been given the red-crayoned letter, then he stopped, turned shyly round and called out.

At first Ghote thought he had not heard what had been called. But then he realized that there had been only five words and that he had registered every one of them.

'He wore red check shirt.'

They were not much. But they did confirm a little one of the contradictory statements that Superintendent Karandikar's interrogators had obtained from the witnesses to the actual snatch. There had been talk of a shirt, either red or blue, either checked or striped. But the consensus had on the whole been for a red checked shirt and here was a gramme of confirmation.

Clearly, too, it was the most the news-vendor was going to be able to give by way of help. But, feeling that some tiny thing had after all been accomplished, Ghote went round the block to the front entrance and its luxurious lift, feeling a degree more optimistic.

★   ★   ★

Up in the penthouse again Ghote found that Manibhai Desai, after the sharp warning about fingerprints he himself had given the day before, had done nothing at all about the new note. It lay in its envelope still on the scatter of newspapers on the floor of the hall.

Stooping down and lifting it with one fingertip at each opposite corner, Ghote examined it. But the plain envelope and the rough red capitals yielded nothing. He went over to the rosewood laminate table where the telephone was and dropped the letter on to it. Then, taking his penknife from his pocket, he succeeded in teasing up the flap of the envelope without touching the rest of it.

After that it was easy enough to slide the note inside on to the table and unfold it.

It consisted of a single sheet of very ordinary writing paper, identical as far as Ghote could remember with that of the first note now undergoing, for what it was worth, laboratory examination. And as it lay on the luxurious-looking surface of the table its message, in the same brutal red crayoned capitals, was plain to see:

YOU HAVE CONTAK PELICE—WE MITE BEEN KILLING BOY BUT WE STIL HAVE SOM HART LEFF—GO TO GREAT WESTERN HOTEL AGEN AT 8 TO DAY MORNING

Pidku was alive.

That thought swept warmly through Ghote's mind in advance of his swift, cold consideration of the situation presented by this renewed communication with the kidnappers. Within instants he was busy trying to work out whether matters were now essentially any different from what they had been before something somewhere in the enormous extent of Superintendent Karandikar's bandobast had betrayed to the kidnappers that the police had been brought into the affair. On first consideration he thought that things had not changed: the kidnappers still held Pidku, from the new note it appeared that they still were making their appalling claim for the huge sum of twenty lakhs for his life, and they had begun again to set up a rendezvous to collect it.

So it was simply a question of Mr Desai going to the squalid Great Western Hotel once more and then taking to a new rendezvous the one lakh, or another such sum which doubtless could be got together by the efficient Mr Shah if Mr Desai had not received back the notes Superintendent Karandikar now held. They would have, too, to repeat their plea to the kidnappers to settle for this sum and to think of Pidku's father, but there should not be any difficulties about that.

But what about Superintendent Karandikar? The immediate temptation was simply not to tell him about this new development. Then no interference of his would ruin Mr Desai's generous gesture. And, after all, he had said that confidence between him and the proprietor of Trust-X Manufacturing was at an end. Yet to keep the news from him would plainly be a serious dereliction of duty.

Was there a way out that would satisfy both the insistent claims that the missing Pidku made and the older, more rational calls that sprang from all his years as a policeman?

There was. But it did not come at all in the

152

way Ghote had expected. It came from the tall figure of the manufacturer of Trust-X standing beside him. He too had been reading those crude capitals. And drawing his own conclusions from them.

'Yes,' he said now, 'it is as I had thought from the beginning. No one would be so cruel in their heart as to kill that boy. So this is first-class. First-class.'

He rubbed his large, well-manicured hands briskly together.

'What we must do immediately,' he continued, 'is to inform the good Superintendent Karandikar. This will give him just the advantage that he needs. In no time at all, if he listens to my advice, we will have those rogues behind bars.'

'But— But—' said Ghote. 'But the superintendent said that all confidence between you has ceased to exist.'

'Yes, yes,' said Manibhai Desai. 'Always when a person is at fault he attempts to attack. But in business you must never allow such an attitude to irritate.'

He reached across the stark note and its envelope and picked the receiver off the white telephone.

'What number should I ring for the superintendent?' he asked.

Ghote told him, and as the rich man's long

153

finger worked swiftly round the dial he put to him a hesitant question in addition.

'Mr Desai, are you still willing to provide the sum—that is, the amount—er—the sum that you previously mentioned?'

The ringing tone from the telephone sounded out clearly in the light-filled hall.

'One lakh of rupees?' said the proprietor of Trust-X with total briskness. 'Certainly not. There will be no need for such ridiculous steps as that. There never was. Those men will do nothing.'

The insistent ringing tone was answered.

*   *   *

Ghote could not bear simply to stand there and hear the proprietor of Trust-X come to terms with Superintendent Karandikar. He might have gained a sneaking pleasure from hearing a superior officer who had so consistently abused and distrusted him having to take high-and-mighty instruction on how to do his job. But when it came to it he found he hated to hear a civilian tell anyone in the force how to go about their job, and especially was it galling when the person being told had after all a deserved and envied reputation among all his colleagues for efficiency and success.

154

So he stepped away and looked round the spacious hall, its expensive Mizrapur rugs and its sun-filled windows with their as yet unrenewed yellow velvet curtains. The pile of folded newspapers was still lying on the floor and he stooped to pick them up.

As he did so he saw that the attempted kidnapping of little Haribhai, son of the manufacturer of Trust-X, 'the tonic you owe to your loved ones', was no longer a matter to be kept quiet. The story, showing evident signs of being a last-minute scoop, was on one of the front pages.

To divert his mind still more from the exchanges between Mr Desai and Superintendent Karandikar—they had now reached the stage of swapping flowery compliments—he began to read. The story had nothing unexpected to contribute, but it was plain that most of the facts of the affair were now public property. And naturally they were of passionate interest to the paper. The customary aloofness of its news columns was more than once breached. Adjectives spattered. 'Agonizing', 'cruel' and 'heart-stretching', all were pressed into service to describe the dilemma of such a public figure as the proprietor of Trust-X Manufacturing. Was he to exercise 'his manifest generosity'—someone had even acutely

155

remembered the previous day's large contribution to the fund for the Bihar Flood Victims—or was it to be 'not the least shade of compromise with such miscreants?'

But at last Manibhai Desai had ended his negotiations with Superintendent Karandikar.

'Yes,' he said, putting down the telephone receiver and looking across at Ghote, 'most satisfactory. The superintendent and I have agreed that this new rendezvous at the Great Western Hotel must be kept. But on this occasion the superintendent has decided, at my advice, to act on a smaller scale altogether. I understand he failed to get the necessary co-operation in his moves last night. However this time I do not think we will be troubled with communication breakdowns.'

'And you are hoping to lead his men from the Great Western Hotel to whatever new rendezvous you are given?' Ghote asked, feeling a sort of careless despondency knocking from side to side in his head.

'Yes, yes. The superintendent expects a further rendezvous to be set up for a time very shortly after the call. However we have agreed that there is no need whatsoever to allow these anti-socials to set the pace. I would tell them that I cannot raise the

156

necessary sum till at least eight pip emma tonight, and that will give us full time to co-ordinate the whole operation.'

'I take it,' said Ghote, with continuing depression, 'that this is a ruse altogether, and that you have no intention of raising any sum?'

'No, no, indeed not. There is only one way to treat weak men like these,' the proprietor of Trust-X declared. 'And that is to yield them nothing. Not one anna.'

At the thought of the absolute zero of his forthcoming expenditure a sharp grin split for an instant his wide mouth.

In face of it Ghote nevertheless resolutely squared himself to say what he felt he must.

'Mr Desai,' he began, 'it did not seem to me from the tone of that fellow on the telephone yesterday that these are men who are weak. I grant that they have shown, as they said, that they have some heart still. But all the same it seems to me that they would still be prepared, if driven to it, to commit some desperate deed against the little boy, Pidku.'

'Inspector,' said Manibhai Desai, with a large puffing out of his broad chest, 'I have been most grateful for your support over the past twenty-four hours. But I must tell you that I have not always approved of the advice

157

you have seen fit to give me.'

'But you yourself yesterday feared for the life of—'

'Therefore,' Manibhai Desai came crashing in, 'therefore, Inspector, I think that for us there has come the parting of the ways. I no longer require your services. Go home, and I shall ask Superintendent Karandikar myself to see that you have a suitable period of rest.'

It was the complete dismissal.

'Very good, sahib,' Ghote said.

He turned to the wide front door.

But at that very moment there came a long, insistent and somehow cheerful peal at its bell.

'Shall I open?' Ghote asked.

'Open, open,' Mr Desai said. 'You are not thinking those rogues will attempt to attack me here?'

He gave a ringing laugh.

Ghote, with memories of his own pistol-confronted arrival some twenty-four hours earlier, opened the wide door.

It was the Press.

There were six, perhaps seven, of them, hungry, yapping, even waving their notebooks. Ghote knew, and did not much like, most of them. He recognized in particular an evening paper reporter whom he considered woefully irresponsible in obtaining information regardless of the propriety of its being made public.

He turned to the manufacturer of Trust-X.

'It is the gentlemen from the newspapers,' he said. 'May I offer a word of advice?'

'Gentlemen, come in, come in,' the manufacturer of Trust-X said, the scent of publicity suddenly and plainly heady in his stallion-wide nostrils.

'Sahib,' said Ghote urgently, 'you would remember that it would not be till tonight that Superintendent Karandikar would be swooping on these men once more?'

But the proprietor of Trust-X had ceased to pay him any attention. Sadly he went over to the lift, whose gate the journalists had left open, and set off for the ground.

As the silver-walled cage plunged him swiftly downwards, his spirits sank as fast. Surely Manibhai Desai in his present frame of mind, all the businessman, and Superintendent Karandikar, smarting from a setback and doubly determined to exercise the utmost, cold efficiency, surely together they made a combination that would fail altogether to remember that at the heart of the case there was a little boy of five years of age, torn away from his home, with a life that would be so easy to snap?

159

CHAPTER TEN

An unexpected day at home did not bring Inspector Ghote the pleasure it ought to have done. He could not rid himself of the thought of little Pidku, presumably shut up in a back room in some crazy, overcrowded part of the city, bewildered, perhaps ill-treated, suddenly taken away from all that was familiar to him. Even the very domestic comforts unexpectedly at hand served by contrast only to nag at his sense of unease.

He quarrelled with his wife.

When he had arrived out of the blue she had said something about there not being anything for him to eat at midday. He knew really that she had spoken in joke, although there was not in fact any food actually cooking. But something in him, some stubborn desire to make himself miserable, had driven him to take the remark as being seriously meant. He had replied, though he knew perfectly well that it would be quite easy for Protima to prepare something quickly, that if she was unable to cook for him he could go and get a meal at the Elite eating-stall nearby.

And Protima, who was looking a little tired

as if she had not in fact slept well the night before, had not laughed him out of his over-dramatized bitterness, as at other times she might have done. Instead she had taken his mention of the Elite, a place they had often poured scorn on together for suspected dirtiness and adulteration of its dishes, as a personal insult to her cooking and she had told him to go there if he wanted. And this had made him determined not to go out, though he could see that Protima was now also determined to do nothing about getting anything ready to eat.

So when the time came to eat each of them got rapidly more hungry and equally rapidly more bad-tempered.

It was then that Ghote, following a private train of thought, abruptly asked whether the new supply of Trust-X, which he had sent for in good time, had arrived. Protima snapped out that it had not and that Trust-X Manufacturing was always bad about sending the new month's supply and that this indicated that there was no reliance to be placed on the product in any case.

Ghote wanted to reply that she was saying this only because, now that he had been able to reveal to her that it was the proprietor of Trust-X, no less, who had been the subject of his case, she was getting at him personally and in addition playing on his long-held, irrational faith in the tablets. But he knew that to mention this would be to expose more of his thoughts than he really wanted, and so he kept silent. And this made him yet more irritable and even more determined to find something to accuse Protima of.

For most of the afternoon he was not very successful in this unpraiseworthy aim. But eventually he found something of a stick to beat Protima with: his Ved seemed to be late coming home from school.

'How many times have I told that you must see he does not linger?' he snarled.

'He is four minutes late only,' Protima answered. 'And even that is if he had come as quickly as he could. Cannot the boy be allowed to talk with one friend even?'

'That is just what causes the trouble,' Ghote pounced in. 'Two boys start to talk. Then one proposes a game. And the next thing is they are far from home and some evil person sets eyes on them.'

'But Ved knows well he is not to talk with evil persons.'

'How can a boy of that age know when a person is evil? There are so many dangers. So many people who would do any wicked thing to obtain a few paise only.'

He knew perfectly well that his Ved was

sturdy and reliable. He knew that he always got home in the afternoon within a set quarter of an hour. But the thought of Pidku darted thin spears of pain into his mind, sometimes easing, sometimes worsening, never stopping.

'I had better go out and look for the boy,' he said, putting on an air of righteousness, and knowing he was doing it.

'Well, go if it pleases you,' Protima answered. 'Ved will like to see his Pitaji for once.'

'He will not like so much when I meet him,' Ghote retorted. 'He will not like to get a beating.'

And he stormed out of the house.

He met Ved just beyond the gate of the little, scrubby garden of the box-like Government Quarter house that was his home. The boy was with two friends, but he broke away from them at the sight of his father.

'No, no,' Ghote said perversely, though he had been touched to the core by this sign of preference, 'I have to go out. Do not leave your friends.'

He walked off down the road in the direction of the despised Elite eating-stall at the corner, with its wooden benches and crude wooden tables and its big brass cooking-pot always wafting out a smell that was at the same time both appetizing and nauseating.

And what would he do now, he asked himself. He would have to end the pretence and go back home in a few minutes, and then Ved would be hurt that his happy advances had been spurned. Should he take a cup of tea at the Elite? And risk getting ill? He owed it to Protima not to do that when he could have all the tea he wanted in his own house just by asking for it.

And then, mercifully, the thought of buying an evening newspaper occurred to him. It would make a perfect excuse for his outing. Generally he avoided buying a paper for economy reasons, but today the purchase would be justified on the grounds of his needing to know if there were any developments in the Desai case.

But even now, still attached to the last traces of his sulkiness, he refused to let himself get the paper he preferred but paid out instead for the one that employed the reporter he particularly disliked. And this was how he came to see that Manibhai Desai's decision, made 'in the best interests of little Pidku', to trick the kidnappers with a false ransom was being broadcast far and wide some three or four hours before it was due to happen.

He saw at once what must have occurred. Manibhai Desai had refused to listen to the warning he himself had given him that among the reporters at the door of the penthouse there was at least one from an evening paper, and had simply assumed that they were all from morning papers. Thus he had confidently and brazenly disclosed the ambush plan.

What would happen? Ghote stood in the full sun with the paper, whose opening two paragraphs alone he had read, held out in front of him. Would the kidnappers perhaps fail to see this particular paper? It was possible, of course. To judge by the spelling of the two notes they were not great readers. And yet that spelling and those capital letters, so crude as to be only marginally useful as handwriting evidence, were they possibly only a disguise adopted by the clever mind behind the whole affair?

There was still that business of the accuracy with which the kidnappers had fixed on twenty lakhs as the ransom sum to be accounted for. It might be purely a coincidence, but on the whole it argued that there was someone involved who would be capable of making researches into the financial standing of Trust-X Manufacturing.

And certainly the man who had scrawled those red crayon capitals, if they were not a disguise, would be far from capable of digging out figures like that. And then there was the elaborateness of the first scheme to get hold of the ransom money, too. Whoever had devised it had, in point of fact, defeated Superintendent Karandikar. And the man who could do that was no everyday goonda from the chawls somewhere. So, if there was an intelligent head of the gang keeping well out of sight—he might perhaps be a man with a full-time job who would have to leave last-minute details to the crude individual on the telephone—then it was more than likely that he would be reading every newspaper he could get hold of to check on each new development.

And if he had read this . . .

Ghote found that the sun-reflecting white sheet between his two outstretched arms was violently trembling.

He shook his head, retreated to the dense shade of a nearby neem tree and, rapidly folding the open sheets of the paper, applied himself to a detailed study of the rest of its story on the Desai case.

What he came to read first sickened him and then frightened him.

Preceded by a formal denial, the reporter

had regaled his readers with the suggestion that the whole kidnapping had been planned by none other than Pidku's father. It was, according to the story, all an elaborate plot to extract money from a universally known benefactor.

And the worst part of the whole business was that, although Ghote had seen for himself the old tailor's reaction to that fantastic demand for a fortune of twenty lakhs in exchange for the life of his son, yet the piling up of facts and half-facts in support of the theory began in the end to sap at his belief in the absolute innocence of Pidku's father. After all, he caught himself agreeing, the tailor had been employed apparently for many years by Manibhai Desai's first wife as well as his second, so he was bound to know a good deal about the family's habits—and perhaps even about their ability to pay just twenty lakhs, he added in spite of himself— and then there was, too, the business of the two children changing clothes. Could that, as was suggested, have been part of the plot? A cunning scheme to relieve the kidnapper of the difficulties of keeping captive an awkward and demanding boy like Haribhai Desai?

Abruptly Ghote felt a need to see his own son. He wanted somehow a reassurance that

167

innocence rang true. He left the compact shade of the neem tree and almost ran through the hot sun to his house.

As he entered the little garden with its few ragged marigolds drawing a wilting existence from the already dusty soil he heard the telephone begin to shrill.

'I am here, I am here,' he called, and raced inside.

It was the proprietor of Trust-X.

'Ah, it is you? It is you, Inspector Ghote, at last? Please to come. I have asked also for Superintendent Karandikar, but you I want especially. Something terrible has happened.'

★   ★   ★

The proprietor of Trust-X had refused point-blank to say what the terrible thing was, though Ghote had been able to get out of him that at least there had not been a successful attempt to snatch the plump and fierce little Haribhai. When he had said that it would take him some time to get to Mount Greatest, since he had no car, he had been commanded immediately to 'take at once taxi, at my expense, my personal expense'. He had done as he had been asked and he had sat in the back of the taxi anxiously gulping a few hastily grabbed bananas.

So it was not long before once again he was shooting up the whole height of that luxurious block in the silver-walled lift and ringing again at the bell in the wide teak door of the penthouse.

A servant opened to him, recognized him and said that his master was waiting in the drawing-room. He swiftly ushered Ghote through.

Superintendent Karandikar, stiffly upright and greyfaced as ever, was already present, though it looked as if he had arrived only moments before. But when Ghote entered the big, airy room with its blue raw-silk-covered sofas, its wide shaded picture window, its rich red wall-to-wall carpeting, its radiogram and discreet refrigerator, the tall proprietor of Trust-X abruptly turned away from the superintendent and came towards him almost at a run.

'Inspector Ghote,' he said. 'Inspector, thank God you have come.'

'What is it?' Ghote asked, his heart pounding at the look of transfixed misery on Manibhai Desai's boldly-marked features.

'They have sent—'

The manufacturer of Trust-X stopped. He shut his deep-set eyes for an instant, screwing them up as if to prevent himself getting the least glimpse of something. Then he made an awkward, badly-aimed gesture in the direction of a low, round, glass-topped table not far from where Superintendent Karandikar was standing.

'There,' he said. 'There.'

Ghote, unable to think what to expect, went over.

He saw a small package, roughly torn open. Its stiff brown paper lay like a big, open, brown-tinted lotus flower on the pool that was the table's surface. At the centre of the paper was a small collection of straw, matted, dirty and broken, looking like the nest of a small and inefficient bird. And on that there was a sheet of white writing-paper with that familiar scrawl of red crayon capitals on it. But this Ghote only half-saw. What seized and gripped his attention the moment he realized what he was looking at was a little, worm-like, darkish thing lying on the white writing-paper.

It was, slightly crooked, the little finger of a boy of about five years of age.

'I telephoned just now to a surgeon at Grant College who is a very great friend of mine,' said the proprietor of Trust-X in a voice that sounded hollow and small. 'He promised me that it would not be a matter involving great pain.'

Ghote passed his tongue over his dry lips.

'It is what it looks like?' he asked. 'The little finger?'

'There cannot be any doubt about that, man,' Superintendent Karandikar said with a sharpness that Ghote welcomed as if it were an acid lime he had thrust into his mouth on a day of tense thundery heat.

'In any case,' said Manibhai Desai, 'the father is coming. There is—'

He pulled out a large white silk handkerchief and wiped his long sloping brow.

'There is a scar, just higher than the knuckle,' he said. 'He would be able to confirm.'

'Yes,' said Ghote.

He forced himself into rational thought. The note? What did it say? He stooped and, avoiding looking too closely at the worm-like finger, read.

SO AGEN YOU CONTAK PELICE— THIS IS TO MAK YOU BELEEF—EF YOU WANT PAY NOW PUT YELO CLOTHE OUT OF WINDO AT FRONT

The proprietor of Trust-X saw what he was doing.

'Already I have hung one of the yellow curtains from the hall out of the window there,' he said. 'I suppose they would have a watcher somewhere below. He could be

171

anywhere.'

'What?' exclaimed Superintendent Karandikar, pouncing. 'You mean to say you have done that already? You have given in to these people?'

'When I have seen that,' Manibhai Desai replied with dignity, gesturing with his large right hand towards, but refusing to regard, the thin brown crooked tube of flesh on the thick, soft writing-paper.

'My good man,' the superintendent said, perhaps smarting under the patronage he had received earlier, 'you must not think that a mere show like this means our friends intend any real mischief. They could get a good stiff term of RI for this certainly, but for men of that type rigorous imprisonment is not so very rigorous. But they know well that if they kill that lad we shall find them, and then one Thursday morning up at Thana Gaol it will be the rope for the lot of them.'

Ghote knew that, in a way, what the superintendent had said was plain good sense. There existed a strong deterrent to a cold-blooded killing such as the kidnappers threatened in sending that tiny, pathetic little piece of a human body there in the packet. But such cold reasoning seemed wrong to him in face of the picture lodged in his heart of a small boy, aged only five, with little

172

pudgy baby-hands still, on one of which now there would be a tiny bloody stump.

But he realized that to make any sort of appeal to the superintendent would be hopeless, and even exceeding his duty. So instead he endeavoured to find something to say that would establish in the superintendent's mind an image of himself as a calmly efficient officer. Then perhaps he could suggest in some way that they should go through with the process that Manibhai Desai had begun when he had hung one of his golden-yellow hall curtains out of a window.

'This package,' he said, with as much briskness as he could muster, 'we must send it as fast as possible to the lab people. There is a good deal of material involved. There may well be something for microscopic examination to show.'

'I suggest, Inspector,' Superintendent Karandikar said drily, 'that the messenger who brought the packet is a damn' sight more likely to provide us with some answers than any up-in-the-air scientists.'

'He is here? You have caught him?' Ghote said.

'Yes, Mr Desai was telling me when you arrived. It was a boy, and he had the good sense to refuse to let him go. I am going to carry out an immediate interrogation.'

'Of course, sir,' Ghote said. 'But, all the same, may I send for transport to take the packing materials to the lab?'

'Oh, do what you like, Inspector,' said the superintendent. 'But I think you would find that, when I have finished with this messenger, there will be no need of laboratories. Or of treating with criminal elements.'

And he gave the proprietor of Trust-X a look of cold hostility.

CHAPTER ELEVEN

Manibhai Desai had detained his captive in a built-in store cupboard near the kitchen of the big penthouse. On the way to this temporary prison he explained the circumstances of the boy's arrival.

'He is young only,' he said. 'About twelve years, I should say. And just a street boy. But he had the cheek to come up in the residents' lift—how he dodged past the chaprassi I cannot say—and then when he rang at the door he insisted to see me myself.'

'You did well to detain him,' Superintendent Karandikar admitted. 'It sounds as if he may indeed be an active accomplice. However, soon we shall see.'

He rubbed his hands briskly together.

'He told he had been given money to put the package into my hands only,' Manibhai Desai said. 'So, as soon as I heard that, I guessed who it might come from straight-away, and I put the little blighter under lock and key.'

Standing now in front of the blank door of the cupboard, he took the very key from his pocket.

'Are you ready then?' he asked.

'Certainly,' said the superintendent. 'It will not take long to deal with his sort of nonsense.'

Manibhai Desai inserted the key. Ghote took a pace backwards and prepared himself to counter any attempt to escape.

The proprietor of Trust-X turned the key with a snap and flung the cupboard door wide.

There was no rush to break out. Instead Ghote and the superintendent were confronted with the startling sight of a boy of twelve clad only in a pair of torn shorts who was bright blue in colour from head to foot.

'Come out,' said Manibhai Desai, evidently not at all as amazed as Ghote by this extraordinary colour.

The boy stepped lightly forward. And, in the better light, it was plain to see that hair, face, naked ribby torso, tattered shorts, legs and bare feet were all a shining and exuberant blue.

And it seemed that Superintendent Karandikar, for all his tigerish efficiency, was as much disconcerted as Ghote. Because instead of sharply launching into his promised lightning-speed interrogation, he jabbered out a series of almost incoherent questions.

'That colour? That blue? Why is it? What

176

do you mean by it?'

The blue boy answered with a grin.

It was a grin of clear simplicity, softly lighting up his whole blue face. And suddenly Ghote, no doubt because the colour reminded him of that used in pictures of the gods, saw the boy as a young Krishna, the embodiment of prodigal, unthinking love. But the answer he gave was as ordinary as could be.

'It is the factory,' he said. 'We are living next to the factory where they are making powder for sprinkling on people when it is the day of Holi. Whatever colour they are making all the people near get on them. This month was blue.'

'Where is this factory?' Superintendent Karandikar barked, safely back to being the unerring interrogator.

Unhesitatingly the boy gave him the name of the factory and of a street in the Bhuleshwar area where it was situated. And in answer to the next question he described where his home was and how he lived there with his four sisters and widowed mother.

'Get on to a telephone,' the superintendent snapped at Ghote. 'Ring this Holitints place first. Check everything. Then get a car over there as fast as you can and have the mother brought in to Headquarters—if she exists.'

He gave the blue boy a look of unrelenting suspicion, but in return received only a smile of dazzling purity. And, during the half hour following Ghote's telephone calls, he was not able once to shake the boy from the simple story he had to tell.

A man had come up to him, a man wearing a red checked shirt, aged between twenty and thirty, of medium height, with no distinguishing marks. He had given him the packet and precise instructions about how to deliver it. But he had not taken long to say what he had to say, and he had chosen to carry out the transaction in the deep shadow of the narrow lane next to the colour-powder factory. So it had not been possible to see much of his face. He had spoken Marathi, the boy's own tongue. And finally he had given him one 50-paise piece and had said that when he got back there would be another for him.

'Where are you to meet him?' Superintendent Karandikar pounced, all claws.

'Nowhere, sahib,' the boy said, giving his sun-shining smile again. 'He said he would find me.'

'Hm,' grunted the superintendent.

A look of quick guile flashed into his eyes.

'The coin,' he snapped, 'where is it? Produce it.'

The boy dipped two thin blue fingers

178

inside the cotton strap at the top of his blued-over shorts and a moment later drew out a glinting, silvery 50-paise piece. He looked at it with glowing eyes.

Wealth.

The telephone rang and Ghote, at a quick word from the superintendent, went to answer. It was from Headquarters. They had picked up the boy's mother. She confirmed his existence and said that, as far as she was concerned, he was playing with his friends somewhere.

'Tell me something,' Ghote said to the CID sergeant he was talking to. 'This woman, is there anything strange about her?'

'Strange? No. Unless that she is a shade of blue from head to foot. But that is from a colour-powder factory there. The whole place is blue.'

So they let the blue boy go.

He went, plunging unconcernedly down into the dark shaft of the servants' stairway, a rubber-bouncing, joy-scattering element to the last. And, as the three of them stood on the landing after he had disappeared waiting for the lift to come up and take Super-intendent Karandikar down, something-perhaps of the urchin's unclouded touch-stone happiness must have penetrated deep into even the sparely upright tiger-figure of the

179

superintendent himself. Because, without any preamble, he abruptly favoured the proprietor of Trust-X with an observation.

'It is the other fathers,' he said. 'It is them I have to keep in mind the whole time.'

He seemed to think the remark, enigmatic though it was, needed no amplification.

But, to Ghote's relief, Manibhai Desai quite quickly broke the grimly imposed silence that followed it.

'Other fathers, Superintendent?' he said. 'I am afraid I am not following.'

The superintendent shot him an iron-grey, unyielding glance.

'Fathers whose children may be kidnapped in the future,' he explained brusquely. 'May be kidnapped, or rather, I say, will be. Will be kidnapped, Mr Desai. If anybody in Bombay city is allowed to get it into his head that here is something they can get away with.'

'So the tailor must, if necessary, suffer?' Manibhai Desai asked, after a pause.

But the superintendent gave him no answer.

They waited, a silent trio, for perhaps a minute longer, until at last the steel doors in front of them parted with oiled smoothness and the silver-walled waiting lift was revealed.

Manibhai Desai made no comment either

as he and Ghote re-entered the penthouse and established themselves in the big, airy drawing-room under the golden gazes of its two sunburst clocks. But barely had they done so when a servant came in.

'It is the tailor, sahib,' he said to the proprietor of Trust-X. 'He is saying that it is you he must see and not this time the Memsahib.'

Mr Desai jumped up with sharp decision from the plump and deep silk-covered sofa where he had just flung himself.

'Yes,' he said. 'It is I he must see. Bring him. Bring him now.'

Ghote found himself filled with a sense of almost unbelieving wonder. Was this the man who only a few hours before had refused ever again to offer even a single rupee to ransom Pidku? Was this the man who earlier had been so unwilling to allow his heart to respond to the call made on it that he had passed on to someone else the task of telling the father a huge sum had been demanded for his son? Was this the man? The man who was now insisting on himself breaking the news to the tailor that his only son had been, in all probability, brutally mutilated?

Ghote glanced over towards the glass-topped table where that terrible, straw-packed little parcel still rested, opened up

like the nest of some ugly disruptive bird. So
unlikely were the words he had heard that he
almost expected to see on the glass surface
only a big jade ashtray or some other
luxurious knick-knack. But no, there, stark
with all its blood-cruel message, the packet
lay. And Manibhai Desai was proposing to
tell the victim's father what it contained, and
to ask him to verify that the atrocious act was
exactly what it seemed.

'Sahib?'

It was the tailor. He was standing as he had
done the day before only just inside the door,
and he was looking too quite unchanged by
disaster, even to the enormous and minutely
neat darn at the very centre of his singlet.
And again he was asking, in a voice of the
most gentle respect, what it was that he had
been summoned for.

'It is you,' the manufacturer of Trust-X
said, looking him slowly up and down.

There were tears in his rich voice.

'*Ji*, sahib.'

'There is—there is a terrible thing I have to
tell you.'

Manibhai Desai's bold features seemed
actually to be less well layered with flesh than
they had been when he had dismissed Ghote
not many hours earlier. Would he be able to
carry out his self-imposed vow, Ghote

182

wondered. Or would it once more fall to his own lot to tell the father what had happened to his son?

But the proprietor of Trust-X was clearing his throat to speak again.

'It is your son. It is Pidku. He is well. He is alive. But they have—'

Again a terrible check. And again the proprietor of Trust-X forced himself to go on.

'What I must tell you is that those men have— They have cut off a finger.'

And then, now that it was out, the almost incoherent babble of assuagement.

'It may not be him. There may be another child, a dead child perhaps. I do not know. But if it— If it was, then already I have asked a doctor—consulted—most eminent—met at charity function. It would not have hurt much. It would not have hurt him much.'

Manibhai Desaï's right arm shot out in a stiffened gesture, as if he were a stern schoolmaster pointing to a pool of ink on the floor.

But the rigid forefinger was directed, like a held-out stick, at the untidy little nest on the round, glass-topped table.

And, slowly, without a word, almost circuitously, the tailor made his way across the red wall-to-wall carpeting towards it. His progress, on lined and cracked bare feet, was quite silent. But it nevertheless made as

183

much effect in the big, airy room as if a shouting, demonstrating *morcha* was parading and protesting down its length.

And then the tailor was there, at the table. He bent forward from the waist. His hand came up as if he was going to stretch out and pick up that little brown crooked worm of flesh lying in the centre of the ragged nest. And then his arm dropped dully to his side. He leant an inch further forward.

For a long ticking-out of time he peered, and then slowly he straightened his back and turned towards the manufacturer of Trust-X and Inspector Ghote.

Ghote saw that from underneath the tape-mended lens of his spectacles a single tear was trickling down the side of that parched, aged-before-its-time face as, wordlessly still, the old man left them.

Manibhai Desai's question had been answered. The little scar above the knuckle of that small tube of flesh had delivered its message. It was beyond doubt Pidku's finger that had been sent to them. And, Ghote thought, it was now beyond doubt too—how could he have ever given room to the slightest of doubts?—that there was no truth at all in that vile suggestion in the paper that the tailor himself was the master-mind behind the whole affair.

And then the telephone rang.

For a long moment neither Ghote nor Mr Desai was able to react properly to the sound. It was as if it was an intrusion of whose nature they could know nothing.

Ghote was first to recover. But he lifted the receiver still feeling himself to be in a remote world.

'Yes?' he said hollowly.

A voice spoke at the far end. A flat, familiar voice.

Ghote clapped his hand across the telephone mouth-piece.

'It is them,' he jerked out, all alertness now. 'It is them. The kidnappers.'

Manibhai Desai came over with clumsily hurried strides and took the receiver.

He had barely had time to give his name when the flat voice cut in. Ghote could not hear the exact words, but the tone was plain. Curt orders were being given.

'But—but listen...' Mr Desai said after a while.

The voice ignored him. It spoke a few words more.

'Yes,' said Mr Desai. 'I have got a suitcase. I used it when—'

A sharp interruption.

'Yes, yes, I will. It is in leather. It is quite old. It comes from the office, they have it for

185

carrying amounts of cash. It is what is called a Gladstone. It opens in the middle instead of having a lid.'

Another terse question.

'It is brown, yes. Brown leath—'

A burst of instructions. And then that click of finality that meant that once again contact with the men who had cut off little Pidku's finger had been lost.

'What did he say?' Ghote burst out.

'It is to be near the Gateway of India,' Manibhai Desai answered, his deep-set eyes already looking into the future he was speaking of. 'It is to be at Apollo Bunder tonight at 7 p.m. I am to wait under the statue of Shivaji with the money in that bag you heard me describe. And at some time it would be taken from me.'

His right hand abruptly opened in a wide gesture as if it was already letting fall the intolerable burden it had had to carry.

Ghote forced the policeman in him to the surface. What new elements had been put into the situation by this move from the other side? He had rapidly to concede that their idea was a clever one. He could see what the scene would be like round about the big triumphal arch of British days. There were often hundreds of people there. And just after darkness had fallen it would be even

186

easier for some inconspicuous idler to pass in front of the figure of the proprietor of Trust-X, standing alone underneath the big statue of the horsed Shivaji, and to snatch that bag crammed with money. Then they could pass it rapidly to a confederate and perhaps on to yet another, then on again to a waiting car or taxi, or even drop it into a motor-boat puttering past the high quay. It could be spirited away within a couple of minutes. And who among the crowd of strollers of all sorts, among the sellers of postcards and of pens, among the furtive, tourist-seeking money-changers and the clamorous fortune-tellers, among the vendors of roast peanuts, of coconuts, of crushed sugarcane, of chick-peas, who might not be one of the kidnap gang in disguise?

They did not really know at all how many of them there might be in total to operate such a scheme. So far they had had descriptions, vague and part contradictory, of two men only, the one who had soft-talked the two children, who had been wearing probably a red checked shirt, and the driver of the getaway car, bearded certainly but possibly a Sikh or possibly a Muslim and, according to the Turk-like little Haribhai, without any hands.

Either of these might be the one who had

spoken on the telephone, the possessor of that flat voice. But surely there was also at least one other person involved, the mind at the back of the whole enterprise, the mind that had chosen this crowded and difficult place for the second attempt to pick up the ransom money, the man who had defeated Superintendent Karandikar's great bandobast. And such a man might easily have at his command twenty others to take part in some complicated manoeuvre among the evening crowds in the chancy darkness of Apollo Bunder, half-lit by the naphtha flares of the vendors' stalls.

'How much?'

Ghote came back with a jerk from his reverie. The proprietor of Trust-X was putting a question to him. And, as he returned to reality, he realized with a feeling of suddenly acute panic just what that question was and how utterly impossible it was for him finally to answer it.

How much? How much should now be offered to the kidnappers to release little Pidku? Well, sums could be discussed perhaps, if the matter was treated carefully. But the question itself ought not really to have even been raised. Because overriding it came the question of whether any money should be offered at all. Or, more precisely, whether Superintendent Karandikar, cold protector of those 'other fathers', ought not to be informed about this new development as soon as he had got back to Headquarters. If he was, it would mean, Ghote had no doubt, a firm, explicit and immediate order that the brown Gladstone bag should once again contain only dummy notes. But he himself felt by no means convinced yet that this was the right course. Something in him revolted at it still.

'Sahib,' he said cautiously to Manibhai Desai, 'the matter of money is something that you are bound to discuss with the police, since we have been introduced into the affair.'

'But I am discussing,' Manibhai Desai said. 'I am discussing with you.'

Ghote would have liked to have accepted this. He forced himself to speak again.

'With Superintendent Karandikar.'

The words came out in a hoarse choke.

Immediately the proprietor of Trust-X flushed up.

'With that man I am not discussing,' he said, his voice rising. 'Already he has been responsible for such cruelty to that boy.'

'But he is my superior officer,' Ghote answered, bleakly forcing himself on against the beating of his will.

'You must forget all that,' Manibhai Desai

said, his bold features shining with fervour. 'The time for orders and chain of command is gone. Those evil men would stop at nothing. It might have been my little Hari that they had taken.'

The vision of that little Turk in the hands of the kidnappers in place of the beaten-down tailor's Pidku for a moment distracted Ghote. He felt then that he might have had another view entirely of the situation if the domineering Haribhai had been the victim. But at once he knew that this was not so, that, however unlikable a child Haribhai was, here were things he ought never in any circumstances to be subjected to.

Yet still he could not allow himself fully to agree with Haribhai's father.

'No, sahib, I am sorry,' he said obstinately. 'I am a police officer, and it is my duty to report developments in a case to my superior.'

'Listen,' Mr Desai replied, flinging his arms wide. 'Listen. I am needing you. You can resign from the police.'

'No. I am a policeman.'

'Then go on being a policeman. Be a policeman for Trust-X Manufacturing. We are getting to be a concern on such a large scale that I can no longer oversee all myself. There are departments already I have not visited for months, even when they are doing new things. There is Regional Ordering. There is Goods Outward. I am needing a trusted assistant to check such places. Come. Come.'

A broad and rosy avenue opened before Ghote. He longed to take it. All his dilemmas of this moment would be ended. He would in all probability better his financial position. He should be able, in such a job as Mr Desai was holding out, to act as he felt he ought, as he could not do now.

And then black fogs of doubt planted themselves in his way. To act as his better feelings dictated? When he would have to carry out the behests of the owner of Trust-X manufacturing? No, there would be occasions in plenty when clashes arose there. To give up the way of life that was implanted in his heart as surely as the feelings he now had for poor, protectionless Pidku?

'No, sahib. No. It is not possible.'

'Then you can get out. Go. Go. Go.'

Ghote stood squarely.

'Yes, I will go if you no longer require the assistance I was assigned to give,' he said. 'But go or stay I must do my duty and inform Superintendent Karandikar as per earliest convenience of developments to date.'

CHAPTER TWELVE

Ghote stayed. The proprietor of Trust-X gave in, with very bad grace, and Ghote made his call to Superintendent Karandikar informing him in full of the latest telephone call from the kidnappers and its new rendezvous at the Gateway of India. And, during the period of something less than two hours before the new drop was due to take place, he was busy enough.

He supervised the despatch to the CID laboratory of the bird's nest parcel and its terrible tiny contents, and telephoned at length to explain the urgency of dealing with it as quickly as possible, cunningly invoking the name of Superintendent Karandikar— 'you are to report to him personally'—to ensure priority treatment. He also assisted the proprietor of Trust-X in checking over a new lakh of rupees brought in person by 'my Accounts Department', or the much-tried Mr Shah. This new sum they added to the original lakh which Superintendent Karandikar had released, not without reluctance, now that he had been informed of the kidnappers' latest move. And they wrote too another note in almost the same terms as the one Superintendent Karandikar had found in the white box, begging the kidnappers to accept this lesser sum.

Altogether it was an uneasy time. Mr Desai never lost the resentment that the turning-down of his offer of a post with Trust-X Manufacturing had aroused in him. When Superintendent Karandikar rang to explain the arrangements for ambushing the new drop-point he stood beside Ghote at the telephone and hissed awkward directions at him every few seconds.

'Tell that I have put paper in the bag only, not the two lakhs.'

'Say something so that he would think the lakh he sent back has gone to office safe.'

'Say I will not have any of his men at all near me beside the Shivaji statue.'

Obediently Ghote relayed these requests, suitably modified. And obediently he relayed back the counter-requests of Superintendent Karandikar.

'You will inform Mr Desai he is not on any account to move from his place under the statue.'

'Tell Mr Desai he is to hold hard on to the case when the attempt is made to grab it and at the same time he is to signal with his free arm.'

At this, of course, Manibhai Desai had

193

retorted for Ghote's own information, that he was going to do everything in his power to shelter whoever would seize the bag. Ghote thought it most prudent to bring the call to an end as rapidly as he could.

Nor was the situation in the penthouse made any easier by the arrival, from a Lions Club Bridge drive in aid of the 'Help the Handicapped' campaign, of Mrs Desai.

'Not a word about all this,' Manibhai Desai muttered to Ghote as her ringing voice was heard from the hall berating a servant for not coming more quickly.

But the very first thing Mrs Desai wanted to know when she came into the drawing-room was whether 'this nonsense about the tailor's boy is over and done with yet'. Her husband, by way of reply, indicated Inspector Ghote.

Ghote contrived to say something about 'steady progress is, however, being made'. And then he had to listen to a lecture, which he felt to be somewhat justified, on how lower-grade public officials always avoid giving direct answers to questions. He might have accepted it without too much inward concern had it not ended with a pointed reference to the Commissioner and his wife.

Mrs Desai even moved towards the refrigerator cabinet as if to take the telephone and ring her patron there and then. But her husband strode across and placed his tall frame between her and the instrument.

'Please,' he said, 'there may be important call just coming.'

'It is from those men? They are asking for more money?'

'No, no, no, no. It is— It is a business matter only.'

'Business at this time? It is quarter past six already.'

'Yes. Yes, it is late. But— But I have had to tell Shah to stay on in his seat. He is behindhand with his figures once more. The state of affairs in Accounts is disgraceful. Disgraceful. He has asked even to have assistant.'

It seemed, however, that denunciations of Mr Shah were an excuse that rang true. Because Mrs Desai declared, with a shrug of her lithe and elegant shoulders, that 'in any case I have no time to be talking this and talking that, I have to find something to wear tonight.' And off she went.

So Superintendent Karandikar's final call detailing the last of his arrangements was received without interruption.

'A small force but a good one,' he barked down the line to Ghote. 'Every man briefed by myself in person. Every man knowing to the last footstep what his task is. Security one hundred per cent. I myself in on-the-spot charge of all operations for the whole of Apollo Bunder. And you, Inspector, from your position in the chauffeur's place of Mr Desai's vehicle in constant visual contact with me. I shall be wearing the disguise of a Moslem woman in a burqa.'

'But, Superintendent— But, Superintendent sahib, how shall I tell it is you when you are covered from head to foot in black?'

'Do not interrupt, Inspector, when I am giving you your orders.'

'No, sir.'

'I shall be dressed in a burqa, but I shall also be carrying a bundle wrapped in orange cloth. Orange is the best colour for long-distance observation, Inspector.'

'Yes, sir.'

'The bundle will contain my personal walkie-talkie, keeping me in full touch with every aspect of the case wherever it occurs.'

'Excellent, Superintendent. A first-class stroke, sir.'

'In the event of unexpected moves I shall be able to order immediate counter-action. I do not think that case of false bank notes will get very far, Inspector, even if it leaves his hands.'

'No, sir. I shall see you at the Gateway then, sir.'

Ghote looked across at the top of the big radiogram on which there rested the Gladstone bag, safely containing packet after packet of real fifty- and hundred-rupee notes. Mr Desai followed his gaze.

'We must go,' he said, looking up at one of his sunburst clocks. 'It is twenty past six already.'

'I think we ought not to leave too early,' Ghote replied, wondering nevertheless whether he really needed to oppose the proprietor of Trust-X once again. 'It is possible that the superintendent will have some last-second orders still.'

'But what if there are traffic delays?' Mr Desai said, moving over anxiously towards the money bag.

'Half an hour is more than time enough to reach the Gateway only,' Ghote answered, finding himself determined, against his own beating, inner inclination, to act in the calm manner Superintendent Karandikar would expect.

'I think we should go now,' the manufacturer of Trust-X said, with an excess of his formidable coldness.

'I am sorry, sahib, I must await any possible final orders. But I will go and make sure I have your chauffeur's cap and coat.'

The white, high-buttoned coat and the white cap with the glossy black peak had been ready in the hall for the past hour, waiting to be snatched up. But Ghote knew that to stay in the same room as Manibhai Desai now was to risk another explosion.

Outside in the hall he stood and waited. It was not very likely really that Superintendent Karandikar would ring up again with some last addition to his orders, though it was possible. But what he really hoped, he recognized now, was that somehow the superintendent would undergo a change of mind and that he would ring to say that if the proprietor of Trust-X really wanted to let the kidnappers have some sum of money then he could do so.

Yet if the superintendent did do this, as he never would, he would as likely as not be wrong, Ghote acknowledged sadly to himself. When all was said and done, the rational thing was to refuse to give in to grasping and evil men. Even if the kidnappers were going to be given as much as the whole twenty lakhs that would put Trust-X Manufacturing on the verge of financial collapse, they would quite possibly simply demand yet more. With men without principle, as men who would steal a child must be, there could never be any safe dealing.

And yet . . . And yet . . .

But then the telephone did ring.

Ghote, quite forgetting that one of Mr Desai's cherished swarm of instruments was in the hall, rushed back to the drawing-room. The manufacturer of Trust-X had already picked up the receiver.

'Yes? Yes?' he was shouting. 'What is it?'

Ghote stepped up beside him to take the call, unable not to hint in his attitude at a slightly contemptuous coolness, though he was far from feeling cool.

Would Superintendent Karandikar possibly after all allow the soft alternative?

And then he heard the voice coming from the receiver. It was not Superintendent Karandikar's: it was the flat tones of the spokesman of the kidnappers.

'Change of place to meet. Go instead in car to GPO. Have the money beside you in back. Tell chauffeur to drive all the way to KEM Hospital. Go by Crawford Market, Bhendi Bazar, Nair Hospital and Victoria Gardens. Somewhere you would be stop. Leave at once. Now.'

The far-end receiver was jammed sharply down. Nerves were once again stretched in the enemy camp.

Manibhai Desai looked at Ghote. Ghote

looked back at him.

'He said to depart straightaway,' Mr Desai proposed, sudden elation shining in his deep-set eyes.

Ghote gave one brief spurt of thought to Superintendent Karandikar and all the men he would have already mingling alertly, yet perhaps conspicuously, among the evening crowd round the Gateway of India. Quite soon now the superintendent, his spare and upright form draped from head to foot in the unlikely thick black flowing folds of a burqa, would be taking his place among them. Perhaps he had already left to do so, and would be at this moment out of contact...

Yet on the other hand the black burqa-clad figure was to carry a large orange bundle. And that bundle was to conceal a two-way radio. So the superintendent could be informed of this sudden switch in the kidnappers' plan, a deliberate device no doubt to avoid just the sort of ambush he had set up. He could be informed. But only at the cost of some delay. And the kidnappers had said 'Leave at once'.

So to do what Mr Desai, with a gleam of freedom in his eyes, had just proposed and to leave this very moment would not be altogether acting in an unreasonable way.

The notion hovered. And then into his

mind there came again the vision of that long, jagged-edged butcher's knife and the milky soft flesh of a five-year-old's throat beneath it.

He ran across to the long, low-slung radiogram, gave Manibhai Desai a swift grin of complicity and snatched up the money-filled Gladstone bag.

★　　★　　★

Darkness came just as Ghote brought Manibhai Desai's big Buick up to the massive pile of the General Post Office building, approaching it from the south after a wide and hurried sweep down from Cumballa Hill and round through the Fort area of the city so as to start the itinerary the kidnappers had set from its very beginning. It was possible, he reasoned, that they intended to make their bid for the Gladstone bag here at the very start where there was plenty of traffic and the chances of a jam holding up the Buick were about 100-to-1 in favour.

Indeed, as he took the big car round to the left so as to pass the ornate, palm-blotted façade of the VT Station, there were three separate occasions when he was forced to a halt. At each one he delayed as long as he could—once in fact till the irate man at the

201

wheel of an Ambassador behind him blared hard on the forbidden horn—but no one slipped out of the jostling crowds on the pavements, as he had half-expected, jerked open the car's rear door and grabbed the stout brown leather bag.

Up along to Crawford Market, past the tall office buildings, darkened now, and past all the hectoring billboards with their clamorous messages in English, Marathi and Gujarati, there was no opportunity to stop. But in the gloom of one of the long arcades here would one of the kidnappers perhaps be waiting to check that the Buick had gone by in accordance with their orders? Perhaps they would.

At the gap in the opened glass panel behind his head Manibhai Desai's face loomed forwards.

'What if they had wanted to make their attempt just now?' he asked.

Ghote shrugged his shoulders in their white uniform coat.

'I do not think they will risk the car having to stop by chance,' he answered. 'What we have to look for is something done deliberately to cause a stoppage.'

'Yes, but what could that be?' Mr Desai asked, anxious as a child about to get a mysterious treat.

'It would be easy enough to arrange,' Ghote said. 'They could half-block the road somewhere ahead where it is narrower with someone carrying out unauthorized automotive repairs. Or even easier, they could arrange a false breakdown. Every day my colleagues in the Traffic Department are complaining: one breakdown and there is a jam that can last half an hour or more. And you know how often cars go wrong.'

Behind him he detected Manibhai Desai wagging his head in serious agreement.

'That is why I am always buying foreign,' he explained. 'It is difficult sometimes over spare parts, and expensive, but...'

Ghote hardened his face into a proper chauffeur's impassivity at this and concentrated on the traffic snarl ahead where the flow of vehicles both ways along Carnac Road crossed their path.

Would it be here that the kidnappers could rely on a car that was making its way northwards having to stop? But no. Irritatingly the lights ahead turned green and they got across and into Abdul Rahman Street without actually having to come to a halt.

Well, Ghote reasoned, with the thicker masses of people spilling on to the roadway from here on, in the way they always do in the living quarters of the city, there would be plenty of opportunities for a forced stop. A vendor's barrow pushed out in the road and deliberately overturned, some sort of false procession got up at a cost of a handful of rupees, anything.

He sent the big Buick pushing slowly forward past the crowds emerging from the open-fronted shops and spilling out on to the roadway. Cyclists swerved and swayed in front of them. Handcarts piled high with sacks or bales of cloth impeded the already jerky traffic-crawl. It would be easy enough for someone to break into a run and jump up on to the car here.

But no one did.

Bhendi Bazar and the intersection with the wide, cross-city thoroughfare of Sardel Patel Road. People were even thicker here, milling this way and that, some hurrying, others dawdling, pairs of men hand in hand slowly loitering. The stream of cars, lorries, buses crossing their path was more thrusting than anything they had yet encountered.

Is this where I would do it, Ghote asked himself. It was about one-third of the way along the route the kidnappers had laid down. They would have had time enough, if they had wanted to, to check that their rules were being obeyed, to see that there were no obvious signs of a police escort and then perhaps to telephone to a point ahead and give the all-clear. But, on the other hand, in the stretch yet to come conditions would be perhaps even more favourable for stopping a car.

And it seemed that this must be the kidnappers' reasoning. Although the Buick was held up for almost five minutes waiting to get across into what Ghote still thought of as Parel Road, though it had been officially re-named Victoria Garden Road, there was no attempt to make contact.

They made slow progress forwards. Ghote felt obliged to drive with the window beside him fully down so that if anyone wanted to give him an order to pull in, or even to turn off, there would be no difficulties placed in their way. So he caught the full force now of the dust and the odours impregnating the air all around, drains stench, sweat smell, dung-fire reek. In his ears there racketed the noise of a thousand jabbering, shouting voices, the grinding roar of low-gear car engines, the bang and batter of carts and handcarts and of horses' hooves and bullocks'. But he forced himself to keep alert, glanced continually from side to side, waited for the sign to come, whatever it would be.

They had entered the Muslim quarter and

left it behind them, and now they had reached an area of taller, more fearsomely leaning houses. It seemed there were even more people to the square yard than before, and more noise and sharper smells of dung, filth, garlic, spices.

They were going at a snail's pace, actually pushing aside with the big car's front fender people in the roadway and the occasional mooning, rubbish-chewing cow. It was the perfect place. There would be no trouble at all here in opening the rear door beside Manibhai Desai and telling him to push out the Gladstone bag. There would be no difficulty in melting into the mass of humanity all around, once it had been taken. Pursuit by anybody would be almost out of the question.

And nothing happened.

The tall shape of the Parsi Statue. And the point where they had to snake right into the part of the old Parel Road now called Dr Ambedkar Road. Once again a tangle of traffic brought them to a complete halt. And once again there was no attempt at taking delivery.

Had the kidnappers bungled it? Had they meant to make contact earlier and by some sheer chance been foiled? Were they even now trying to pursue the slowly moving

Buick?

Ghote peered and peered into the rear mirror. But all he could see was a confusion of bodies and faces, of vehicles and barrows in the jangle-lit darkness.

Victoria Gardens passed by on their right, Byculla Station and the bulk of the Railway Hospital on their left. They came to an area where the houses were bigger but old, battered and past all their glory. From their entrances people by the hundred seemed to be pouring. The soft masses of old banyan and pipal trees blotted out the lights.

Suddenly Ghote became convinced of the way it would be done. There was bound to be a tree sooner or later that jutted out over the roadway. Say someone was lurking in its branches, ready to drop down on the car's roof?

He awaited the heavy thud above him.

But it seemed that it was not going to come.

He twisted round for a moment and spoke to Manibhai Desai.

'Sahib, perhaps it would be better if you were to lift up the case and put it on your knees. So that it can be seen by anybody.'

'Yes, yes, I will do that.'

The manufacturer of Trust-X was as pathetically willing to please as any one of his most debt-ridden minor suppliers.

Slowly the big Buick forged its way onwards. The fork to the right at Chinchpokli Road passed by. More than two-thirds of the journey had gone now.

What if they had made some mistake, failed to see a signal? Would the kidnappers take that for a brutal gesture of refusal? And would they make their own infinitely more brutal reply? Again Ghote saw the jagged edge of that imagined butcher's knife and the pipe-thin neck it menaced.

Ought he to have persuaded Mr Desai to make his offer bigger? Would he have come up with three lakhs if a really forceful case had been presented to him? Or two and a half lakhs? Surely that little more the manufacturer of Trust-X would have granted easily enough? And it might make all the difference.

If it got to them.

Half a lakh. That little more, though a whole year's earnings, even for someone doing well in the commercial world. And in the other tray of the scales, a life.

Into the area illuminated by the big car's sidelights an old woman, bent almost double, with a sari faded to colourlessness wrapped round her gnarled and fleshless limbs, almost failed to move herself out of the way. A life?

What was one life in the middle of all the dying round them now?

Yet Pidku had to be saved. That he knew. Knew in the region where the analyses and comparisons of the brain were at total discount.

And now the very last stage of their journey. Ghote took the big Buick across the traffic stream for the fork right into Government House Gate Road. Some half-mile more and they would be there.

When were the kidnappers going to claim those two lakhs that waited for them? And it could never have been more than two lakhs. There had not been time to have added even a thousand rupees more since he and Manibhai Desai had become allies on little Pidku's behalf once again.

A straight stretch of road now, with the going better than at any stage before. Perhaps, though, the appointed place would be the very end of their journey?

Yet he dropped down into first and kept the big car at a silly, steady, chugging crawl.

Ahead, a little to the left, the huge shape of their destination could be seen now. Was someone waiting in hiding under the shadow of the big hospital's outer wall? Was there a motor-scooter, say, with its engine already running ready to weave in and out of the traffic and the crowds in a fast get-away? Would next the Gladstone bag on its rear carrier be snatched off at the end of its run with shaking, joyful, hardly-daring-to-believe hands? Would it be jerked open? The money counted? Manibhai Desai's new note read? A council of war held? And at last the decision be made to accept that already vast sum and let Pidku go?

At the gap in the dividing panel the proprietor of Trust-X spoke.

'Can you go slower?'

'Sahib, already I am down to five miles an hour only.'

'Yes, yes. I saw.'

With the echoes of that sad voice in his head, Ghote completed at this creeping pace their long journey. He pulled the big car up against the kerb beside the towering bulk of the window-glowing King Edward Memorial Hospital. In silence they waited.

CHAPTER THIRTEEN

It was, as Ghote had finally been sure it was going to be, a fruitless wait in the shadow of the KEM Hospital. After twenty minutes he had proposed that they give it up. After thirty minutes Manibhai Desai had consented, begging only to stay on alone in the car while Ghote went into the hospital and from there belatedly reported to Superintendent Karandikar.

It had not been a pleasant ten minutes at all, standing there in the antiseptic-pervaded hospital entrance hall endeavouring to speak quietly into the telephone with white-uniformed nurses clicking by on sharp heels and occasional doctors giving disdainful, suspicious glances at this impertinent uniformed chauffeur in their midst. Superintendent Karandikar had been every bit as hostile as Ghote had expected, and it had been a considerable time before Ghote had been able to convince him that only the extreme urgency of their departure from Mount Greatest had prevented him reporting the change in the kidnappers' plan. Eventually, after listening to a long and forceful account of the penalties that awaited

211

anyone who failed even in the spirit of their duties when they came under Karandikar, Ghote had managed to secure a grudging acknowledgement that this time he had not apparently betrayed the letter of his orders. But the whole experience had left him feeling drained to the core.

And then they had set out for home again, cutting across south and west as quickly as they could towards Cumballa Hill. It had been almost entirely a time of depressed silence. Only once had Manibhai Desai spoken.

'What do you think they will do now?'

A plaintive question. Ghote's answer had been as cheerless.

'I suppose they will get in contact again, probably by telephone. It is the only thing they can do.'

Nor was their reception at the penthouse any more encouraging. Mrs Desai came out into the hall to greet them. And she would not even listen to her husband's feverish inquiries about whether there had been any calls.

'So you are back?' she said to him. 'Back after leaving me with no explanation to give for you not being here.'

Manibhai Desai's boldly handsome features took on them a look of offended

212

anger.

'And am I having to say where I am going always?' he demanded. 'Am I a child only that I have to tell I am going here, I am going there?'

'And when it is the wife of the Commissioner of Police himself who is inquiring?' Mrs Desai retorted, her long, red fingernails flicking in a gesture of contemptuous triumph.

The proprietor of Trust-X assumed an expression of instant wariness. His wife was quick to see she had the advantage.

'Yes,' she said. 'It was Meena who rang and asked what you were feeling about the matter. And what could I reply? I found that you had gone. And then, when she asked to speak to the CID man the Commissioner had sent to keep a guard on your little Haribhai, I found he also had gone.'

She darted a look of knock-down reproach at Ghote. But she was not going to waste time on recrimination at such a lowly level. Her anger-engorged eyes flickered quickly back to her husband.

'And what was it you were doing?' she said. 'You were trying to pay those men our money.'

There could be no denying that: Ghote was holding the heavy leather Gladstone bag with

213

its stuffed bundles of notes. Manibhai Desai stood looking, for all the boldness of his features, hang-dog. The expression did not placate his wife. Rather the reverse.

'Yes,' she went on, 'always it is you who are thinking you know best. Never are you taking my ideas for publicity for the business. "That is charity only" you are always saying. And it is the same here. You are thinking that you know best how to deal with these men. Pay, pay, pay, it is all you are saying. And all the time it is quite unnecessary.'

'Unnecessary? Unnecessary? They have telephoned? What has happened?'

The proprietor of Trust-X wanted to know. The desire was stamped on deep-set eyes, big pointed nose, wide taut mouth.

'Telephoned? Why should such men telephone?' his wife replied.

'But to make a new appointment. To say what they want. To agree to accept a reasonable sum.'

'Not at all. Not at all. That is not the way to deal with such people. I have told you all along.'

Ghote, standing quietly witnessing this marital combat, noted soberly that this was not strictly true. But Manibhai Desai was too concerned to know what the kidnappers were doing for sober noting.

214

'What new thing has happened?' he demanded in an infuriated shout. 'What new thing? Tell me. Tell me.'

Mrs Desai smiled a smile of panther sweetness.

'But if you had stayed at home you would have heard from Meena herself,' she replied.

'What would I have heard?'

Each syllable was ground out.

'Why, that they have tracked down these men only.'

'Tracked them down? Captured them? Pidku is safe? Is he safe?'

Ghote found, to his burning inner joy, that the proprietor of Trust-X was voicing all the questions he himself longed to pound out.

Mrs Desai turned and walked languidly back into the rich, red-carpeted drawing-room. Her husband, his big teeth clenched in fury at this provocation, followed her.

'Well, answer,' he said. 'Answer.'

'They are closing in on them,' Mrs Desai replied with maddening calm.

'Closing in? Where? How? Are they thinking of the boy?'

Mrs Desai shrugged her elegant shoulders.

'Do you think Meena and I are concerned with the details?' she asked. 'I tell you they have found out somehow where these men are hiding, and the Commissioner has ordered a massive sweep. Thank goodness there is someone to see that a citizen is not treated in this manner.'

For a puzzled moment Ghote could not think which citizen was being treated in what manner. Then he realized: Mrs Desai had been insulted and upset by the attempt on her stepson. And it was she who was being avenged.

And Pidku he found himself thinking savagely. Was he to be sacrificed to placate Mrs Desai?

But the about-to-be-avenged lady had not yet finished with her erring husband.

'In any case,' she said with loftiness, 'you can find out everything for yourself, man-to-man.'

'What do you mean "man-to-man"?'

'Just that I have promised you would ring the Commissioner himself as soon as you got in.'

Mrs Desai paused, savouring her victory.

'I have promised you will ring,' she added, 'and tell the Commissioner that you have stopped all this ridiculous business of wanting to protect these wicked and greedy men.'

Manibhai Desai's pushingly handsome face took on instantly a look of deep, though secret, obstinacy.

216

Ghote, his senses tuned to an ever more acute pitch by the pressure of all that had happened since he had first heard about little Pidku, was able to analyse what the proprietor of Trust-X must be feeling as if it were his own heart that was involved. He had pledged himself to pay out for Pidku, but to what deeper extent was a man such as he pledged to a wife twenty years his junior? And here, there seemed, was a chance being held out to him to believe that the newer, more urgent promise could be satisfied while the older debt was still honoured. But what was this hope that the affair was suddenly near its end? How reliable was what Mrs Desai had said about the kidnappers having been located?

These, Ghote knew, must be the questions Manibhai Desai was asking himself. And they accounted perhaps for that look of reserve. He certainly was not going to go back to the hard line on the strength of what might be only wild words of his wife's. But neither was he going to reiterate his stand on Pidku.

Ghote saw now that once again the boy's fate was in the balance. No one would or could pay for his eventual safety except the manufacturer of Trust-X. And now, despite all the firmness of resolve that had been implied by his decision to tell Pidku's father himself about the contents of that grisly package, once again his resolution was faltering.

But was it faltering with right on its side? If what Mrs Desai had told them really did come from the Commissioner himself, then there must be a good deal of truth in it. And, if so, there really might be no need after all to pay the kidnappers.

Yet what could have happened to put Superintendent Karandikar on the men's traces? And, if he was closing in on them, was he the sort of man who would give proper attention to little Pidku's safety at the moment of confrontation?

Manibhai Desai, who had stood mutinously glaring at his wife, abruptly turned away and shouted for a servant in a voice tingling with suppressed fury.

Evidently echoes of the high-raging domestic combat had already reached the servants because the door was opened with give-away suddenness and the Desais' No. 1 bearer presented himself.

'Get me a drink,' the proprietor of Trust-X ordered. 'Whisky, a big one.'

The man padded softly over to the imposing walnut and chrome cocktail cabinet that stood under one of the sunburst clocks

218

and took out a tumbler and the whisky bottle.

'I will have a drink also,' Mrs Desai said. 'Bring it to me now. A whisky too. And hurry, the burra sahib has to make telephone call.'

'No, I do not,' Manibhai Desai countered immediately.

'Hurry with my whisky,' said his wife to the bearer, on whose face Ghote was able to observe a tiny delight at this drama unrolling just above his head.

'Hurry,' Mrs Desai repeated. 'The burra sahib wishes to use the telephone.'

Manibhai Desai's face took on a look of doubly pent-up rage. He strode over to the cocktail cabinet like a bull in full reckless charge and brushed the bearer aside.

'Here,' he said. 'I will fix myself.'

He seized the whisky bottle and tipped a hugely generous quantity into a second tumbler. Then, actually snatching the siphon out of the bearer's hands, he splashed a short spurt into and around his own glass, lifted it and drained it in one.

Mrs Desai took her drink from the little silver tray on which the bearer had proffered it and then walked over to the refrigerator. She stood beside it and gestured with an elegant, red-nail-tipped hand at the white telephone beside her. She did not say a word.

Manibhai Desai glared at her. But then suddenly a little brutal smile lit his deep-set eyes.

'Well,' he said, 'I am tired. I am exhausted. It has been one hell of a day for me. I am going to bed now.'

His lurking smile broadened into triumph. He gave his wife a full, unabashed look.

'And kindly not to disturb,' he said.

Followed by the bearer, whose back was pantomiming a much over-stated show of discretion, the proprietor of Trust-X strode from the room.

And left Inspector Ghote alone with Mrs Desai.

Ghote, who during the whole of the lightning-flashing confrontatation between the Desais had stood not far from the door into the big room, remained where he was. He said nothing. There seemed to be nothing to say.

Mrs Desai also continued to stand where she had been, beside the telephone. From time to time she took a somewhat exaggerated sip from her drink. She posed her free hand on the edge of the refrigerator cabinet, her red nails catching the light, in a gesture of nonchalance so stiffly languid that it made her seem immovable as a carved dancing-girl.

Watching her, Ghote began to feel acutely

thirsty. He had endured that long, stinking and hot drive out to the KEM Hospital and he found he wanted nothing more now than a long cool drink. Buttermilk, iced. That would be the very thing. And no doubt the refrigerator contained, among much else, a good supply of buttermilk, deliciously cold and refreshing.

Abruptly Mrs Desai left her post and went over to the radiogram. She began, again with a show of idleness worthy of a film star, to flip through the pile of records on one side of the long, low cabinet. But suddenly her doubly obvious constraint put a notion into Ghote's head.

Up till now he had thought of Manibhai Desai's wife as being no more than a vivid, jerky, implacable force aimed at keeping every rupee of the Desai wealth in Manibhai Desai's pockets. Yet could she be as totally single-minded as that? Evidently she had feelings. Why else was she so embarrassed now? So would it not be possible to appeal to the feeling woman?

At the radiogram Mrs Desai had, it seemed, selected the disc she wanted. She was standing reading its label, holding it rather close to her face, vanity apparently forbidding glasses. At any second she would drop the disc on to the turntable and then no doubt blaring music would blot out any chance of a quiet talk.

Ghote cleared his throat. The sound, in the silent room, grated even on his own ears as if it was a bullock-cart crossing a street of cobblestones.

Mrs Desai darted him a glance of fury.

What if she ordered him out? He really would have to go.

'Mrs Desai. Madam.'

She raised a thinly-carved eyebrow.

'Madam, I wish to talk to you. I wish to discuss—Please, Mrs Desai, think of that child.'

Mrs Desai lowered the disc she had been holding so close to her pretty, if tensely so, face. She looked at Ghote with ice-cold disdain. Yet Ghote from his very depths found something which would not let itself be frozen.

'Mrs Desai,' he said, 'I am appealing to you. You have had no children. Perhaps you are not very much caring for children. But, think. To some people a child is a treasure greater than money, than any sum of money. The tailor is poor. Yet I know that in little Pidku he has all the wealth he could desire.'

'What do you talk?' Mrs Desai answered, her voice taking on an edge of lancing anger. 'What do you know of me? Of children? You have no business—'

She broke off. But not because Ghote had interrupted. Something from inside her had blocked the thought.

Suddenly she tossed the record she had been holding over on to the nearest blue silk sofa and strode away across the big room.

'You do not understand,' she said, in a voice so muffled that it took Ghote some moments to guess at the words.

He waited. He had the sense that a whole delicate series of scales and balances was rocking up and down under the crude weight he had dropped into one of the pans, little knowing the complexity of the apparatus he had set in altered motion.

At the end of her long diagonal promenade across the big room Mrs Desai swung round. She looked at Ghote full in the face, her eyes ablaze.

'No,' she spat at him. 'You do not understand.'

I am going to be told to get out, he thought.

'You could never understand. What do you think my life has been? Do you think I have always lived like this? With servants as many as I wanted? With a roof over my head that I know cannot be taken away? I tell you from the day my father, the Colonel— No, no, I will tell you it all, even what I have not told Mani—from the day my father, who would never be more than Captain, shot himself, then I never knew a moment of security until the marriage ceremony with Mr Desai was over.'

Her face, till seconds ago a cosmetic mask of fragile gaiety, showed now cracks and rents of wretchedness.

'Yes,' she said, 'once we had servants, a few. My old ayah, always. But when he died, my father, when he walked out on us, in a few days we had no one. And was I, a little girl still, able to help myself or my mother? And then, then later when I found I did after all have something. Something to take to the bazaar. Then I was determined I would get a damn' good price.'

Suddenly she came racing across to Ghote. Was she going to attack him, the long red nails scratching? But she halted two feet away and thrust that broken pretty face close to his.

'And I got that price,' she said. 'I had to fight. I had to plan. I had to wait. But in the end I married Trust-X Manufacturing.'

There was a hectic blaze in the eyes so close to Ghote's own.

'And now I am enjoying,' she said. 'And he—he has his son and heir. He has

Haribhai, and he is well content. But still I must go on pleasing him. And it is not always so easy. You see me, and I am looking fine. I know it. The hairdresser tells me. The beautician also. But there are times when I do not. When I cannot. And he is older, and other things may get a hold on him. How do you think I can risk having children? How do you think I can risk it?'

Feeling a leaden intrusion in the pit of his stomach, Ghote realized that this was a question he was actually expected to answer.

'I see—I see that—I realize you have difficulties, great difficulties. And I am feeling them. But I am feeling for another person also. For a person with the name of Pidku.'

Mrs Desai did not take her hot eyes off his face. But Ghote looked back at her, gaze for gaze. Pidku, he willed to her. Pidku. A person. A boy. A human life. A life at stake.

And then suddenly the contest was over. Mrs Desai's hot eyes dropped.

'All right,' she said. 'We are both human. If he should need still to pay, I will not stop.'

Ghote felt an absurd sense of happiness. It was as if in boyhood he had been given totally unexpectedly a free ticket to the cinema and a whole sudden prospect of three hours of untrammelled, untouchable enjoyment had

225

spread out before him.

'Well, that is good, that is very good,' he babbled. 'If you would excuse me. I must stay in the flat because they may telephone at any instant. The kidnappers. Any instant. They appear to have missed the last rendezvous they gave, you know. So they may get in contact. But I will go. I will remove myself. Elsewhere in the—'

His incoherent jabber was interrupted by the sharp pealing of the front-door bell.

'Who can it be at this time?' Mrs Desai said, snatching a sort of brightness round her as if it was a garment hurriedly caught up.

'Them,' Ghote said, his heart suddenly pounding. 'Them. They may have sent another messenger.'

He turned and was out of the room and into the hall in an instant. He found the proprietor of Trust-X, his wide-shouldered body in a silk dressing-gown of a deep, magnificent green, just emerging, apparently from his bedroom. He, too, it seemed, had been struck with the same thought about who this late caller might be. He glanced at Ghote apprehensively.

The No. 1 bearer appeared in his turn.

Ghote hurried across and flattened himself against the wall next to the wide front door.

'Please to let him in,' he said. 'I will make

sure he does not leave some message and run away.'

'Yes, yes,' said the proprietor of Trust-X. 'That is the way. Are you ready?'

Ghote nodded his head in agreement.

'Then open,' Mr Desai instructed.

The bearer pulled the front door back with admirable suddenness. Ghote began a sideways sliding movement to get behind whoever should come across the threshold.

And, to his dazzled astonishment, he saw stepping calmly inside the Commissioner of Police for Greater Bombay.

CHAPTER FOURTEEN

Ghote flung out a hand against the wall beside him in an effort to stop his impetus-heavy sideways slide. His clawing fingers did at least slow his body down to the point where his other hand no more than lightly brushed the Commissioner's side.

The Commissioner turned at the touch.

'Ah, Inspector Ghote,' he said. 'I'm glad to see you're still here. I heard that you were accompanying Mr Desai somewhere. It seems you are being of use.'

He gave Ghote a slight inclination of the head and turned his attention to the resplendent, green-draped form of Manibhai Desai.

'My dear fellow,' he said, 'I fear I've dragged you from your bed. I'm sorry. But I was so anxious—Meena was anxious too. And so I said I would come round.'

'Not at all, not at all,' Manibhai Desai said. 'I am always delighted to see you. It is most kind.'

He darted a quick look at his wife. It said 'You wait'.

Mrs Desai did not wait.

'Commissioner,' she said, 'how good of you to come. But I hope I did not give a wrong impression on the telephone. I am standing right behind my husband in all this, you know.'

Manibhai Desai's look of belligerence turned, almost comically, first to bewilderment and then to a tiny flame of trust.

The Commissioner gave Mrs Desai a smile of great warmth and understanding.

'I'm sure you're one hundred per cent behind Manibhai in everything,' he said heartily.

Mrs Desai in turn smiled at him, brightly.

The Commissioner coughed.

'But I have come here to put you both absolutely in the picture,' he said. 'And you too, Ghote.'

'That is most kind, most kind,' said the proprietor of Trust-X, bending a little from the waist and clasping his large hands tightly together. 'Shall we go into the drawing-room? You will take a drink, Commissioner?'

'Well, well, I cannot say that I'm truly on duty,' the Commissioner said with a jovial laugh.

For a few minutes there was much coming and going, with the bearer busily presenting his little silver tray. Ghote found that, this time he was asked what he would have. He eagerly seized the chance of getting his cooling buttermilk. When he had it and the bearer had left, the Commissioner looked all around.

'Well now,' he said, 'this is what I came to tell you.'

The three of them sat forward expectantly.

'We've got these fellows on the run,' the Commissioner announced. 'Definitely. And a smart piece of work it was too, though I say it of my own men.'

What had happened, Ghote wondered furiously.

'Yes,' said the Commissioner. 'I thought when I put my Superintendent Karandikar on to the case that I couldn't have chosen a better man, and now I've proof of it. Do you know what he turned up? The tiniest thing, and I think it's going to put those blighters in the bag.'

Mrs Desai's eyes, in her miraculously restored to fixed prettiness face, widened in appreciation.

'Tell us,' she cooed.

The Commissioner smiled.

'A tiny number of blue grains,' he said. 'That's what caught them. A tiny number of blue grains. When the lab boys on Karandikar's instructions gave that package the kidnappers sent a one hundred per cent check-over, what did they find under the nail of the finger? A few blue grains. Exactly the same blue grains that were on the outside of the package. You see what that means?'

Ghote saw what it meant. He saw everything that it meant. But Mrs Desai was still delightfully mystified.

'No, but Commissioner, you must tell us. This is fascinating. Absolutely.'

Looking at her in a swift access of sourness, Ghote wondered whether the woman he had uncovered in this very room not quarter of an hour earlier had been only a dream, some sort of hallucination.

'Well,' said the Commissioner in a kindly manner, 'it's like this. That packet was brought here by a boy who, we know, lives in the immediate neighbourhood of a certain factory, the—er—the—'

'The factory of Holitints Limited,' Ghote supplied quietly.

'Of Holitints Limited precisely. A factory that blows out over the whole area round a blue powder. Well now, if that same powder was found under the nail of that finger, then it indicates quite clearly that the kidnapped child is being kept somewhere not far from the factory. And you can bet your bottom dollar that as soon as the lab informed Superintendent Karandikar of that he put a

231

full-strength search operation into immediate effect.'

'And they have found where the boy is?' Mrs Desai asked. 'I have been so worried about that poor little mite.'

The Commissioner shifted a little in his raw-silk-covered chair.

'Well, the search is by no means completed yet,' he said. 'These things take a deuce of a long time. Every single house has to be investigated from top to bottom, and you know the sort of warren it is round there. It's a matter of look, look, look and ask, ask, ask.'

'Yes,' breathed Mrs Desai.

The Commissioner drained his glass.

'Well, that's what I came to tell you,' he said. 'And so you can see there's absolutely no need to worry further. No need to—er—parley with those blighters, if you understand me.'

He directed at the proprietor of Trust-X a look of keen inquiry.

Ghote thought he knew what answer Manibhai Desai was going to make. But there was no chance for the words to be uttered. Instead into the big room there came shrilling yet once more the insistent call of the telephone.

Manibhai Desai cast an imploring look at

Ghote. Please, it seemed to say, stop the ringing. Stop it. Let it not now be them.

'Shall I answer?' Ghote asked, getting up and hurrying over to the white telephone. 'We are expecting the kidnappers to call again. It may be them.'

'Yes, yes, man, jump to it,' the Commissioner said. 'I think you're the best one to deal with them. But don't give them an inch. Not an inch.'

Ghote picked up the receiver. Before he had even time to say hello the voice he had been sure he was going to hear was speaking.

'Mr Desai, is it?'

'No,' Ghote began. 'I am—'

'Tell him we could not meet on the way to KEM Hospital. Police wallahs were all round the place where we are. Now listen.'

'Yes?'

Ghote's mind was darting across the facts of the situation almost like a jungle beast fleeing from a fire, skittering wildly from point to point, unable to rest on any solidity.

The first thing was not to say to the kidnappers that there was no longer any question of doing a deal with them. Those blue grains under little Pidku's nail—found thanks to his own insistence on sending the packet for analysis, after all—might mean that the area where the boy was being held had been located. But . . .

But the fact of the finger remained. Those men had hearts callous enough to be able to take a child and cut off his finger. They had the ability to kill. He was certain of that.

Yet with the Commissioner standing behind him, a presence emanating authority, it was a simple impossibility openly to bargain with the caller.

The Commissioner had made it too plain that he backed to the hilt the hard line advocated by Superintendent Karandikar: that to offer money to kidnappers, except with the definite intention of tricking them, was to lay clear the path to an outbreak of crime of frightening proportions.

And there was plenty to be said for that view, too.

But, since the kidnappers were even now calling the penthouse, did this not mean that they had escaped, somehow, Superintendent Karandikar's present search?

It might mean it, certainly. Especially if a new rendezvous was now offered. And if the kidnappers were after all in this stronger position now, then would it not be best to pay them?

At least perhaps an attempt should be made. If the money was taken and Pidku not set free, then it would be a loss. But it would not be the unthinkable thing that would occur if he himself were now to say firmly 'No' and then that jagged knife be drawn across the soft-to-melting child's flesh.

But, even as Ghote's mind darted from point to point in this chain of reasoning, the flat-voiced kidnapper had been giving him the new rendezvous.

'... at nine tomorrow. He is to come alone. No chauffeur. No one. At nine tomorrow morning at the Great Western Hotel again, and there he would be told. And if he is followed, then we would know. We would know and in a moment we would kill. Understood?'

'Wait,' Ghote said. 'Wait.'

But the nervous, hasty man at the far end had jabbed down the receiver—had a squad of Superintendent Karandikar's searchers just passed by whatever shop he was telephoning from?—and Ghote was left with only the bare message.

He turned and relayed it to Manibhai Desai and the Commissioner.

'Yes, yes,' said the Commissioner. 'Tightening round them, undoubtedly tightening round them. It won't be long now.'

'But, sir,' Ghote objected, his voice coming in a quiet gasp. 'But he was able to get out

235

and go to a telephone.'

'Desperate measure, desperate measure,' the Commissioner assured him.

And then the proprietor of Trust-X added his conclusion.

'Yes, I am certain. It is excellent work, Commissioner. Those badmashes are nearly at the end of their rope. It is a good thing I did not pay out, as I had half a mind to do.'

He thrust his hands into the deep pockets of his dark, silk-glowing, emerald dressing-gown and waggled them luxuriously.

'But,' Ghote said in a sudden, awkward semi-shout. 'But you said you would pay. The money is there.'

He pointed to the battered, thick Gladstone bag which was still resting where he had left it when he had brought it up to the penthouse after their fruitless trip to the KEM Hospital.

'Listen, please,' he went on, still jerking the words loudly out. 'Those men have no hearts. If they think they are on the point of arrest they would kill.'

'Nonsense, man,' said the Commissioner sharply. 'They know the difference between hanging and fifteen years RI. They won't touch the child.'

'Commissioner,' the proprietor of Trust-X put in with quietly growing smooth anger, 'I do not think we have any further need of Inspector Ghote. The case is almost cleared up. Those people will not trouble us now.'

'Yes, yes, quite right,' said the Commissioner with quick cheerfulness. 'Whole thing more or less wrapped up. Off you go home, Ghote. Report for duty at midday tomorrow. Dare say your wife will be glad to see you. Got a wife, haven't you?'

'Yes, sir,' said Inspector Ghote.

★　　★　　★

All Ghote could do was to follow the Commissioner's instructions and return home. But with every step depression settled down on him until, well before he had entered the little square of garden in front of his small, boxy Government Quarter house, he was levelled to a hopeless greyness.

Manibhai Desai had dismissed him, and, though once before he had sent him away and then had urgently called him back and begged for his advice, the proprietor of Trust-X was not the sort of person who would go back on a decision twice. Indeed, it had been a wonderful reversal when he had brought himself to ask for help again after rejecting him the first time. Now no hope of such a thing existed.

And did this mean that Pidku was doomed? Back in the penthouse, when he had still been able to be rational about the business, he had argued to himself, while trying to sort out his thoughts in face of the kidnappers' last telephone call, that all was not necessarily lost for the tailor's boy. He had then been able to appreciate the Commissioner's argument that if, say, the searchers bungled the job of making a quick, clean arrest, the kidnappers would not risk making their punishment irrevocable death. Now he could no longer believe that. Greyness prevailed: he felt only that Pidku was bound to die.

Absurdly, too, every little ordinary thing that his tired, groping mind bumped into seemed to be cast in this same hope-lost hue. For some reason the sight of his front door reminded him of the post delivery and from that sprang ridiculously insistent thoughts about Protima's new supply of Trust-X tablets. He felt convinced that they had not come. The fact that the proprietor of Trust-X Manufacturing had backed out of his promise over Pidku seemed to make it certain that his firm too would have backed out of its pledge of prompt delivery. And at the same time, paradoxically, he became possessed of a total faith in the tablets' efficacy that he had never really had before. Without an absolutely continuing supply, he was certain, Protima would simply wither away. A gap of one day could be fatal.

So, instead of creeping into the sleeping house in his usual manner and endeavouring to get to bed without causing any disturbance at all, no sooner had he got in and closed the door behind him than he burst out loudly and anxiously.

'The Trust-X tablets, have they come? Have they come?'

In a moment a startled and sleep-bemused Protima appeared from the bedroom, hugging her white night sari round her.

'Ganesh. What is it? What is it?'

The sight of her a little brought Ghote to his senses.

'I am back home,' he said, by way of rather sheepish explanation for the uproar he had made.

Protima looked at him, blinking with effort in order to clear her mind.

'You are well?' she asked. 'Is anything the matter?'

At once Ghote experienced a sense of quick irritation.

'Of course I am well,' he snapped. 'And what should be wrong? It is just that Mr Desai of Trust-X no longer requires my

239

services.'

He had made a deliberate effort to get this to sound neutral. And he knew it still contained an under-strain of bitterness.

'But he has complained against you? What has he said?' Protima came leaping to his defence, her eyes now beginning to flash and the colour mounting in her high cheekbones.

'It is nothing. Nothing I tell you. And what I am asking is: have those tablets come yet?'

'Tablets? What tablets?'

Protima had been soundly asleep.

'The Trust-X. Has the new supply arrived? You should have finished the old card, even though you forgot one day. Has the new one come?'

'What are you talking? It is the middle of the night. Trust-X. Trust-X. What does Trust-X matter at this time?'

Ghote was at once seized with the most profound suspicions. She had not got the tablets. And already the lack of them was doing her harm. She would not have got into a rage like this if she had taken her regular dose.

'Have they come?' he shouted. 'Have they? Have they?'

And the noise woke up little Ved, who came and stood sleeping in the doorway.

'It is morning?' he asked. 'I am late for

240

school?'

'No, no,' Protima said, sweeping down on him and enfolding him in an over-protective embrace. 'It is the middle of the night only.'

'It is not the middle of the night,' Ghote shouted. 'It is quite early. Quite early. And I am asking where is the new Trust-X.'

'They have not come, Pitaji,' Ved said, his voice more piping for his having reverted in his sleepiness to a more childish stage. 'Mataji was angry when the postman went by and there was nothing.'

'Yes, yes, my little one,' Protima soothed. 'But go back to sleep now. Back to sleep.'

She led him away.

The darkest thoughts filled Ghote's head. The Trust-X had not come. Protima would die. It was certain. And little Pidku would die. And he would be dismissed from the force himself. It was certain.

'And you too should go to bed,' Protima said coming back, and coming back, with typical changeableness, a different woman.

She put her arm round Ghote and shepherded him with warmth to their bedroom. He allowed himself supinely to be led, to be helped undress, to be questioned a little about the appalling events of the day, to be put to bed not knowing what the future held or even what it could hold.

CHAPTER FIFTEEN

An insistent tapping on the shoulder woke Ghote next day. For some seconds he refused to acknowledge that the blotting-out of sleep had ended. He lay willing himself back into conquer-all dreamland. But the tapping—it seemed to be a thin blade being repeatedly brought down on his shoulder—continued insistently, and he realized too that a voice which he had been hearing was not part of his sleep-life, mysteriously and automatically transformable into something that could be dealt with. It was from the outside.

It was Ved. And the words he was chanting in rhythm to the tapping became suddenly clear.

'The Trust-X, the Trust-X, the Trust-X, has come here. The Trust-X, the Trust-X, the Trust-X has come here.'

Ghote sat sharply up.

'What is that you are saying?' he demanded.

But there was no need for Ved to tell him. He saw now that the boy was cluthing in one hand the new square card of Trust-X tablets grouped round their brightly printed dates. It had been this that had been tapping at his

242

shoulder.

He felt a sense of relief, even while acknowledging that his panic about the tablets the night before had been no more than panic, the wild exaggeration of a brain bemused by fatigue and the strain of a long day's nerve-harrowing events.

'And look, Pitaji,' Ved said, 'they have changed envelope.'

'Um?' Ghote answered, sleep temporarily billowing back at him now.

From the front door of the little house Protima called urgently.

'Ved. Ved. I said a moment only. You will be late for school.'

'It is so late?' Ghote called out, feeling suddenly rather cheerful.

'Yes, yes,' Protima called back. 'You said last night that you did not have to go to office till midday. I hope it was right: you were so tired.'

'Yes, yes. The Commissioner himself said.'

Ghote stretched luxuriously.

'Ved. Come on,' Protima called again.

'But, Pitaji look,' Ved said, with fearful earnestness. 'A new colour of envelope.'

And something stirring deep down in Ghote, something unrecognized, made him swing round and seize the envelope Ved had been holding in his other hand. And, the

243

moment he saw it fully, light swept in.

It was an unusually shaped envelope, exactly square to fit the card it had contained. But, whereas hitherto the 'plain cover' under which Trust-X had been sent had been of a good quality, pure white paper, now the firm had descended to using, in the same shape, a very coarse brown paper.

So that this envelope was exactly like the envelope in which the kidnappers' first note had been delivered, the envelope that Manibhai Desai had tossed away and which he himself had worried and worried about and had eventually cajoled the little Turk, Haribhai, to find.

And if the kidnappers' envelope was exactly the same as that in which Trust-X was now being sent, then one thing was likely to the point of near-certainty: that the kidnappers themselves were employed somewhere in the factory of Trust-X Manufacturing.

Ghote's mind started to work with precise rapidity.

First, had the kidnappers in any case already been arrested? Had Superintendent Karandikar's sweep in the area spreading out circularly from the words of Holitints Limited been successful?

'Quick,' he said to little Ved, 'off to school

with you.'

And while the boy hopped and skipped away, understanding without a word being spoken that somehow the envelope he had shown his father had been a good piece of news, Ghote himself ran to his telephone. A quick dialling, CID Headquarters, for once, answering immediately. And the Duty Sergeant's line not engaged.

'It is Inspector Ghote here. Tell me something. Has Superintentendent Karandikar's new big bandobast been successful?'

'Do not make me laugh, Inspector. The whole building is deserted so many men he has on that job.'

'Just what I wanted to know. Thank you, *bhai*.'

Ghote crashed down the receiver.

So the area in which Pidku was almost certainly being held was still being searched. Perhaps in the first flush of triumph somebody had missed some little thing quite near the Holitints factory. And the kidnappers were still unknown, which meant that Pidku was still in danger.

Ghote looked at his watch.

Ten minutes past eight. When in an hour less ten minutes a call from the kidnappers to the Great Western Hotel revealed that the proprietor of Trust-X was not there, as it was bound to do, then Pidku's life would hardly be worth a button.

He ran back and scrambled into his clothes.

Protima came in from waving goodbye to Ved at the corner of the road.

'You are in a great hurry for someone with all the morning to spend at home,' she said.

'No,' said Ghote. 'I am going as fast as I can to the Trust-X factory. If what I have guessed is right, then perhaps I can learn there where those men are holding the tailor's little boy before they discover nobody is going to pay them any ransom and kill him.'

'You think they will?' Protima asked, a quick anxiety springing up in her to match his own.

'If you had seen that finger,' Ghote said, 'you would not have any doubts.'

'Then hurry, hurry,' Protima answered.

And, proof of her involvement, she did not even suggest he should take a cup of instant coffee or a bite of anything to eat.

*   *   *

At the corner of the road, near the Elite eating-stall, he spotted the bright yellow-and-black of a taxi. Battering down all thoughts about how much it would cost, he hailed it and told the driver, a young and wild-looking Sikh, to go as fast as he could to the Trust-X Manufacturing works at Worli in the northern part of the city. He spent the traffic-enmeshed journey not glued to the meter of the cab, though he was twice unable to resist giving it a glance followed by some swift calculation in paise and rupees, but in looking at his watch.

At nine o'clock, no doubt to the second as before, the kidnapper with that flat, threatening voice would ring up the Great Western Hotel from some shop or other—there could be no doubt that men of the kidnappers' sort would not have a telephone of their own—and would find that the proprietor of Trust-X was not this time waiting for the call.

Perhaps he would hang on for two or three minutes. Perhaps he would try ringing a second time. The kidnappers, after all, must be as anxious to get hold of the huge sum they expected Manibhai Desai to pay as the forces of order were to get hold of the kidnappers. But before all that long it would be borne in on the telephone caller that Manibhai Desai was deliberately not keeping the rendezvous. He might then ring through to the penthouse to make doubly certain. But sooner or later he would report to the others that there was to be no money after all. And then what?

A sweat broke out on the back of Ghote's neck as he envisaged the scene. A mutter of angry voices; possibly one of them urging patience—someone from among the kidnappers had written of having 'some heart left' after all—but eventually the decision would be taken; faces would be hardened in worked-up anger; the joint move would come to whatever room or cupboard the little captive was being kept in; and then the quick rush to have it over and done with.

'Faster, faster,' he said to the driver.

The taxi-man, already causing more than his fair share of havoc in the streaming and counter-streaming traffic, became yet more aggressive. Angry shouts wafted after them.

'Do not mind, do not mind,' Ghote said. 'I am CID. I would see you do not get into trouble.'

The promise appeared to carry some weight with the taxi-man and the car nipped, dodged and swayed onwards at the same dangerous rate, weaving through the lines of vehicles, screamingly braking and wildly swerving. But Ghote wondered how well-founded his promise was. He was not working under orders. He was simply rushing on his own initiative to get to Pidku if

248

he possibly could before that nine o'clock deadline.

Deadline, indeed.

But was he justified in what he was doing?

'Shoot those lights ahead,' he ordered the taxi-man.

Justified or not, he was going to go on. He was going to act first, and find explanations afterwards if he could.

The minutes ticked by and mounted up. Ghote forced himself not to let them blot out everything else in his mind. He clutched at the problem that would await him at his destination, a problem so impenetrable that he had not been able before to bring himself fully to contemplate it. But how among perhaps a hundred or more people employed by Trust-X Manufacturing was he to find the one—it might be one only—who had planned this appalling crime against the head of the firm?

The envelope. He must work from that. How was it that this particular envelope had come to be used for the first note to Manibhai Desai? Plainly it had been a mistake on the kidnappers' part, and they had been lucky not to have been tripped by the heels by it before this. Lucky for them that the proprietor of Trust-X was now so successful that he no longer had time to exercise the

249

close supervision of his whole enterprise that had once, it seemed, been his pride. He had mentioned indeed, when making that offer of employment with the firm, that he had been unable for a long time to get round to visiting the Goods Outward Department. So it might well be there that a search for the traitor within his gates could begin.

Someone with access to the new brand of cheaper envelope. Well, it might be possible to do some eliminating there, if only there was time.

Ghote looked at his watch yet again. Already quarter to nine. But at least they were getting near. They were getting near. This was the end of Globe Mill Road.

'Keep it up, keep it up,' he begged the taxi-man.

There ought to be a foreman or somebody like that in the Goods Outward department, and a word from him might reveal in one second the presence—or, more significant, the absence—of some person with a grudge against Manibhai Desai. Then a check at top speed with the Wages department, an address, and he might still at least be on his way before that nine o'clock call was made.

He might. He might. And surely even the kidnappers would not carry out their terrible threat within minutes of the situation requiring it finally arising.

At last the taxi came to a halt at the gate in a high mesh fence that kept the brilliant white, sparkling new factory of Trust-X Manufacturing from contact with the dirt-encrusted outer world.

'From Mr Desai. To see Mr Shah.'

Ghote shouted the words at the tall Pathan gate-man, magnificent in a green turban, finding they came to him without his even having to think. The name of the greasy-suited accountant was the only one he knew among all the employees of the big factory, and so he had produced it. But it was likely that there had been occasions in the past when the proprietor had had reason to send an urgent messenger to the man who summed up in his single person the factory's whole Accounts department.

And it seemed that it was so.

'Straight on, straight on,' the stiff-turbaned Pathan called with a brisk wave of his thick staff.

The taxi drove into the factory compound and drew up in front of the main entrance.

'Wait for me,' Ghote said with urgency to the driver.

It was likely, he reckoned, that if he did succeed in winkling out one of the kidnappers—but how? How was he to find one among a hundred or more in just a few minutes?—he would need to go at speed over to the immediate area of the Holitints factory. So transport had to be assured, and damn the cost.

He ran quickly up a wide flight of steps, through swinging blued glass doors and into the factory's reception area.

Another Pathan, equally lordly in a splendid violet turban stood there. Ghote tackled him in a sheer over-whelming rush.

'Police, CID,' he snapped the moment the glass doors had swung to behind him. 'Your Goods Outward department, where is it? Quick.'

'Through the door to your right, straight along the corridor, then you will see a sign at the far end.'

Ghote, without stopping his onward rush, swung round and charged past a startled-looking girl at a reception desk and through the door the Pathan had indicated. Ahead, a long, wide corridor ran for perhaps fifty yards in a broad, straight path, its floor covered in soft, noise-deadening, squeaky green rubber. Plain wooden doors, painted white, with the names of the various departments on them in square red lettering giving a faintly hospital aspect, were blankly closed on either side. Ghote reached the far end in a little over five seconds.

And there, to the left, was a pair of double doors marked in the same red 'Goods Outward'. They clacked open with a satisfying noisiness as Ghote pushed at them with the palms of his extended arms.

A large hall confronted him, two wide tables or benches running its whole length set about eight or nine feet apart. In the passageway which they formed there were some twenty or more women, busy dealing with supplies of Trust-X in various stages of packing, pushing them along until, at the end of one of the tables, baskets of envelopes awaited delivery to the post office, while, at the end of the other, neat wooden boxes of cards, bundled and tightly stacked, were ready to be taken to shops where the tonic was sold.

Women, Ghote thought, looking down the two rows of industrious, stooping, sari-clad figures. It was a reasonable first bet that no woman was involved in as nasty and heartless a business as kidnapping.

His look swept round the rest of the long, high-ceilinged room. On the outside of the two parallel packing tables various necessary supplies were being brought to the points where they would be used by some eight or nine coolies. One of these? It was likely enough. His eyes raced over the men with their baskets of unfilled envelopes and trays of monthly cards. Was there one with a red checked shirt?

After all, men doing this sort of work did not change every day, or even every week, from a shirt of one colour to one of another. They were as likely as not to possess just the one garment, getting their wives to wash it one night and wearing it again next morning. So a red checked shirted man?

But there was no one.

Who was in charge? A brawny fellow of about fifty with a round, voluble, fat face, dressed in a colourful purple shirt above a bright red dhoti, was moving briskly here and there in the big room. Ghote went quickly up to him.

'Are you the foreman of this department?' he asked sharply.

The big, wide-chested man laughed.

'Oh yes,' he said. 'I am in charge. In charge of a pack of girls and women who leave me no peace.'

His eyes twinkled.

'And the coolies?' Ghote asked. 'They leave you no peace either? They are discontented?'

Again the foreman laughed, richly from the chest.

254

'When they are my relatives only, all but one?' he said. 'No, they have good jobs here, my cousins and my cousins' cousins. We are not having strikes always.'

'And they are all related to you? All but one, you said? What about him? He is an odd man out?'

'Ah ha,' the foreman laughed, and gave himself a double-handed slap on either side of his dhoti-covered belly. 'That one is going to marry my daughter. The last girl I have to marry, and he is going to take her. A good boy, too. A good boy.'

'I see,' Ghote said, with despondency.

He was wondering whether perhaps he ought not after all to ask some questions about the female packers—had he been too simple to think that no woman could act as cruelly as the kidnappers?—when the foreman gave him a quick, acute look from a face still wreathed in smiles.

'But what is all this about, sahib, if I may ask?' he said. 'You seem to think someone here has done something wrong.'

Ghote decided to trust him, a sudden, instinctive plunge.

'It may not be in this department,' he said, 'but someone in the firm has done something wrong indeed, unless I am much mistaken.'

'You are a police, sahib?' the foreman

asked.

'CID,' Ghote answered.

'Then it is this terrible thing that has happened to the tailor who worked for Mrs Desai,' the foreman concluded.

His eyes darkened with concern.

'Exactly. And I have reason to believe that someone . . .'

Ghote's voice trailed into silence. A clear notion of who that someone was had floated abruptly into his head.

The idea may have come from some hidden-away emotional reaction to the warmth of the foreman's personality, or it may have come simply because his mind, having completed its consideration of the kidnapper in the factory as being one of the rough members of the gang, switched to asking whether the person he was seeking might not be the hypothetical master-mind behind the whole affair. But, whatever the reason, the idea had come into being in his head as clear and as definite as if it had been the result of a long chain of closely considered ratiocination.

As, in a way, it was. The salient point in his picture of the supposed master-mind had always been one thing: that someone had fixed with such accuracy on the sum of twenty lakhs of rupees as the maximum possible amount the proprietor of Trust-X would be able to scrape together to ransom his own only son. Added to this there had been the skill shown in the drafting of the various plans the kidnappers had put forward for picking up the money without risking being arrested. But there had also been another element: a hint of indirectness in control. The main plans had been drawn up with skill, but details of their execution— things like the envelope and the occasional indecision shown by the man on the telephone—had indicated more than once a clear lack of close control from the top.

Ghote thought now that he knew why this was. Plainly the kidnappers were operating from whatever place it was, near the colour-spreading Holitints factory, where they were hiding Pidku, but no doubt the master-mind was not able to be there at all times. Quite simply, he had to be at work.

And if he was a senior employee of Trust-X Manufacturing, which of all the people at the factory would know most clearly about the proprietor's exact financial state but the man who in himself constituted the whole Accounts department, the bullied and put-upon Mr Shah?

Ghote, flinging out thanks to the genial foreman, left at a run. With every stride he took he became more and more convinced that the man he was about to tackle would be able to tell him exactly where Pidku, frightened, maimed, five-year-old Pidku, was being kept.

In the brightly coloured, fresh-looking reception area he again demanded directions from the Pathan chaprassi with a sharpness that could not be denied. Yes, the Accounts department was easy to find. It was on the upper floor, just next to the proprietor's own office, and that was directly above them now.

'Through those doors there, sahib. Up the stairs and Accounts you would see on your right.'

Ghote took the stairs two at a time. And with each bounding step he let the anger within himself leap higher.

Then he saw the sign saying 'Accounts' painted on a narrow glass-panelled door ten yards along from the luxurious wood-veneer affair with a board bearing the legend 'Chairman and Managing Director—Strictly Private'. He swerved towards it and, without knocking or giving a moment of warning, he flung it open.

Mr Shah was sitting behind a cheap desk at the far end of a little, high-ceilinged corridor of a room, its walls shelved and heavy with great leather-bound account books. He looked exactly as he had done when Ghote had first seen him two days ago. That greasy suit seemed folded in exactly the same encrusted creases and the very threads at its cuffs appeared to dangle thickly at the very same angles. His large horn-rim spectacles sat in their same filmed-over state at a slightly crooked angle on the small, anonymous nose in the centre of that cross-lined, fleshless, anonymous face.

He looked up, with a quick tree-rat dart of fear, when Ghote stepped into the narrow, book-walled room. But when he saw who it was who had come in his glance dropped again to the long, heavy ledger in front of him and he immediately made an entry in it with the fat old fountain-pen he was holding.

'It is the police inspector who was with Mr Desai,' he said, his mind already more than half fixed again on the columns of figures in front of him. 'It is a message from Mr Desai?'

'No,' said Ghote, clearly and loudly.

He marched up to the small desk and stood glaring down at the accountant across it.

'No,' he repeated, cracking the word down. 'It is you I have come to see, Mr Shah.'

The accountant looked up at him sharply, his eyes peering speculatively up through the grease-filmed glasses.

'Well, Inspector,' he said. 'It is Inspector—er—Ghote, isn't it? Is there truly something that I can do for—'

Ghote banged both his hands down flat on the little, cheap desk so that it shuddered and the telephone at its corner gave a tiny ping. He leant forward until his face was within inches of the lined, cross-furrowed, secretive face of the accountant.

'Where is the boy?' he shouted. 'Where are you keeping him?'

He was able to see, so close he was, the minute flicker of fear in the eyes behind the big, filmy spectacles. The minute flicker of fear, and—was it?—an even more minute flicker of calculation.

'Inspector, is something wrong? I do not at all understand what it is that you are—'

Ghote hit him.

He had not in the least expected to. But the stream of bland words that had begun to slide out in answer to his question offended him like an exquisite insult. And he had swung upright above the little desk and, quick as a lion's paw, his right hand had shot out and landed a heavy blow on the side of Mr Shah's head.

It sent him tumbling from the creaky bentwood chair on which he had been crouching over his long ledger. He fell sideways on to the floor, banging his shoulder against the wall of the narrow room. And he lay there.

'Get up,' Ghote said.

Cautiously the accountant scrabbled on to his knees, his left hand sweeping round in a half-circle seeking the horn-rim spectacles which had flown off the bridge of his nose.

'Where are you keeping the boy?' Ghote demanded again.

Mr Shah got fully to his feet. He had found the spectacles, but he made no attempt to put them on.

'You are assaulting me,' he said.

His voice was steady, and Ghote realized with thankfulness that he had not done him any serious harm. It was not that he did not want to: he wanted to stand over the grimy-suited figure and batter him down time and again to the ground. But he knew that this would only give a defence lawyer ammunition, and besides he was not going to get any information out of his man if he himself was blind with red rage.

So he took a long, deep breath before speaking.

'Yes, Mr Shah,' he said then, his tone as steady as his opponent's now. 'Yes, I am assaulting. You have heard tales of police brutality, I dare say. Well, would you like to

261

find out if they are true?'

'Oh no, you will not,' the accountant answered, his eyes sparking ice. 'I am not the sort you can do that to. I am protected. I work very closely with Mr Desai, Mr Desai who is a personal friend of the Commissioner of Police.'

'Mr Desai,' Ghote countered, still keeping his voice level, 'whose only son you planned to kidnap.'

The accountant's unexpressive face went yet more stonily uncommunicative.

'Inspector,' he said. 'I do not know what wild idea you have got into your head, but I would be very interested to hear what evidence you have for that claim.'

Ghote saw, with a sudden pit of emptiness opening in front of him, that he had rushed impetuously into a very dangerous situation. He had accused a member of the public of a serious offence without a jot of hard evidence to back him up. He had behaved not like a police officer but like an unthinking fool.

Should he try to climb out of it? Say he had not said what he plainly had? Mutter excuses? Cringe and apologize?

But then he knew that he would not. Mr Shah was the person who had planned the kidnapping of Haribhai Desai and, worse, who, when that had gone wrong, had committed the double cruelty of demanding a huge sum against the life of the son of a hopelessly poor man. Evidence might be lacking at present, but he himself had seen the little look of speculation in those eyes behind the greased-over horn-rim glasses and was experiencing now the cold triumph the man was exuding.

Shah was the master-mind. He was. And he was not going to get away with it.

'Mr Shah,' he said, 'you have no need to play these sort of tricks with me. I have reason and good reason to know that you are the man who planned the kidnapping. It is your accomplices who are holding that boy even now. Where are they?'

'Inspector, already I have warned—'

Mr Shah stopped. The greying black telephone on the corner of his cheap little desk was ringing hard.

'Inspector,' he said, 'you can see I am a busy man. I have the whole accounting system of this firm to keep running.'

He gave a pointed glance at the door which Ghote had left swinging open behind him, and reached across the desk for the telephone receiver.

Ghote stood his ground. But the accountant did not allow his presence to put him off. He brought the receiver to his ear and spoke in a clipped businesslike manner that was only a little exaggerated.'

'Trust-X Manufacturing Accounts department. It is Mr Shah speaking.'

'He did not go to hotel.'

CHAPTER SIXTEEN

It had been only six words. But they were enough to change totally the situation for Ghote. Only six words coming distortedly through the earpiece of the greying telephone on the corner of Mr Shah's desk, but Ghote had heard them clearly and had recognized beyond doubt the voice that had spoken them.

It was more excited and disturbed than he was used to hearing it. But it was the flat voice he had first listened to on the telephone in the hall of the Desai penthouse and had heard on four other brutally impressing occasions since. It was the voice of the kidnappers' spokesman informing the master-mind of their enterprise that Mr Desai had not been at the Great Western Hotel to get his instructions for the final rendezvous.

'Later,' Mr Shah hissed into the telephone, the power of his suppressed fury making the hushed word almost into a shout.

He crashed the receiver back on to its rest.

But Ghote's hand descended almost as quickly to clasp his wrist like a steel trap. He jerked it up and twisted it in an instant behind the greasy-suited accountant's back.

'Now,' he said, letting the hatred rip in his voice, 'talk and talk fast, Mr Shah. Where is the boy being kept?'

'I do not know, Insp—'

Ghote gave the arm he was twisting a sharp little jab upwards. The accountant let out a breathy yelp of pain.

'Am I going to force it out of you?' Ghote demanded.

'Inspector, you are making a mis—'

This time Ghote gave the arm a more savage push up towards the shoulder-blade above it. The accountant gave a long, sobbing moan.

'No. No. Stop.'

'Talk then.'

'It is a room behind a paan-shop. In a lane in Bhuleshwar. It is called Bawoodji Lane. It is the paan-shop there.'

A dark song of triumph started up in Ghote's head. He had done it. He had done it. The Holitints factory was in Bhuleshwar. Shah must be telling the truth, and he himself had fought his way to the secret concealed among all the employees of Trust-X Manufacturing.

But had he done it in time? It must be just after nine now since Shah had been told that Mr Desai had not gone to the Great Western

Hotel. No doubt, had that call gone on, Shah would have been asked what the men holding Pidku should do now. Perhaps he would have been asked for his casting vote on whether to kill the boy at once. Well, luckily he had simply told his accomplice to ring back later.

So there ought to be a little time. But there would not be much.

'Right,' he said to the wretched moaning accountant. 'You are going to come with me. And quickly.'

Still keeping an implacable grip on his right wrist, he swung him round the desk and marched him out of the still gaping door. At a sharp trot they descended together to the glossily smart reception area. There, Ghote offered no explanations but simply propelled his captive across the highly polished floor and out through the blue-glass swinging doors. Let the Pathan chaprassi and the elegant receptionist behind her counter make what they would of the firm's accountant departing in this humiliating way. They would soon enough learn the truth about him.

Outside in the bright morning sunlight the taxi was still waiting, the young Sikh at the wheel happily puffing a cigarette. The meter, Ghote thought in an incidental flash, must by now have clocked up a formidable sum.

As he bundled the accountant in ahead of him he shouted an order to make for Bhuleshwar as fast as possible. And then he realized with a little jump of pleasure that now he ought to be able to charge the whole trip to expenses.

*   *   *

For the first part of the journey, plunging southward from the sea-touched spaces of Worli to the close, confined, crowded sweat-pit of Bhuleshwar, Ghote devoted all his energies to extracting from the cowed accountant every detail of his plot that might be helpful in dealing with the other members of the gang in their hideout clustered round little Pidku. He hardly noticed indeed, as his driver swung in and out of the now lessening traffic, that at one stage they had worked their way round Jacob Circle again, within a hundred yards or so of the little Great Western Hotel and its telephone that had figured so prominently in the affair.

Instead he battered without remorse at the greasy-suited Shah. How many others were involved in the business? What were their names? How had they become involved? Ah, so there had also been another of them working at Trust-X. In the stores. And no doubt light-fingered with the supply of new envelopes. Had any of them records of violence? Did they carry any weapons? Had they hidden Pidku in the same place all along? How had they evaded Superintendent Karandikar's searchers? Had they planned to take the boy to a new hiding-place if Mr Desai had agreed once more to pay them? Were they finding it difficult to move about with so many police in the area?

From these and other questions banged out in the swaying back of the taxi, Ghote learnt a good deal. There were, it seemed, only three people involved besides the accountant. The others were, as he himself had suspected, three pretty rough individuals, the storeman, whom Shah had first picked on to help him when he had detected him in a pilfering racket, and two of his friends. They were certainly likely to have weapons of some sort, though the accountant did not think they had any firearms. And, yes by dint of hiding Pidku in a storage box in the garden at the back of the paan-shop they had escaped the massive search that had taken place the night before. And now they had been planning to move on, though they had not thought it would be easy.

'And the boy? And Pidku?' Ghote asked. 'Now that they have not been able to get in

269

touch with you, what will they do?'

'I do not know.'

But the crouching accountant looked so doubly frightened as he said this that Ghote guessed the worst was likely to take place.

'You must know,' he said, putting his face close to his prisoner's and slamming the words into him like blows.

'Inspector, I swear—'

'They have all along been ready to kill? Yes? Yes?'

The accountant put his hands up to his eyes.

'Yes,' he whispered. 'They would kill.'

Ghote swung away.

'Go faster,' he said to the taxi-man.

'Inspector?' Shah said from behind him.

The tone was sickeningly ingratiating. Ghote could hardly bring himself to respond.

'Well?'

'Inspector, it would help if I told you how the paan-shop can be approached from the rear?'

Ghote swung back round on the bouncing, swaying seat.

'Help or not,' he said, not disguising his disgust, 'you are going to tell, and quick.'

'But, Inspector, you saw how Mr Desai used to treat me. Inspector, I was less than a pi-dog to him. Can you wonder I used my knowledge to make him feel?'

The accountant slipped half off the seat in an ecstasy of grovelling. His lined, featureless face twitched and twitched.

'You did more than make him feel,' Ghote said inflexibly. 'You have nearly stamped the life out of another father, a poor man you knew nothing of.'

'But Mr Desai had to be made to pay,' the accountant answered, another terrible twitch distorting his whole face.

'And the boy's finger had to be cut off to make him pay?' Ghote said.

A wild look, raging and flaming, came into his prisoner's spectacleless eyes.

'Yes,' he said. 'Yes, even at that cost. Something was needed to stab him to the heart.'

And the depth of hatred that this revealed, like a black root torn out, made Ghote see that indeed the mastermind of the kidnap gang, for all the cold cunning he had used, had not been set on at the start by any frigid calculation.

Yet, whatever glimpse of sympathy this made him feel for him, he was not going to let his purpose now be deflected.

'You said there was a back way to paan-shop. What is it? Answer up. Answer up, or it will be the worse for you.'

'It is a passage,' the accountant blabbed out. 'It is a passage from the lane that runs parallel. It does not look as if it leads anywhere. There is a pile of rubbish, a chicken coop... But you can get over. And then you are in the gardens between the two rows of houses. It is easy to get from one to the other.'

'And the paan-shop?' Ghote said. 'How do you know when you have reached its garden?'

'That is easy, easy, Inspector. The shop garden is used for storing bales of betel leaves for the paans. There is no difficulty I promise. I promise.'

'Hm.'

Ghote looked at his babbling prisoner without pity. But in a moment he turned and spoke to the Sikh driver.

'Do you know Bawoodji Lane in Bhuleshwar?'

'*Ji*, sahib.'

'Good. Then take the next turning past it, another lane, and stop when I tell you.'

Ghote turned and put his head out of the taxi window.

He was looking for a traffic policeman. What the blubbering Shah had told him about the back way to the paan-shop garden, the garden in which little Pidku must actually be hidden, had given him an idea. If he could

272

hand over the accountant to somebody reliable and at the same time get a message to Superintendent Karandikar to say where the kidnappers were, then he could allow himself before one of the superintendent's heavy-footed squads descended on the paan-shop to slip in by the rear and be ready perhaps simply to protect Pidku, perhaps even to rescue him. If he managed that, while he was at the same time in a position to cut off the kidnappers' retreat should it be necessary, then he would have amply justified his taking of the initiative.

Only, where was there a traffic man? They were not far from Bawoodji Lane now.

Well, if the worst came to the worst, he could tell the taxi-man to stop and then send him to telephone a message to Superintendent Karandikar while he waited himself in the taxi with the acc—

No. There.

Some thirty yards ahead he spotted a traffic constable, a steady-looking veteran with a big grey moustache, a model of neatness and discipline, puttees above his sandals faultlessly rolled, yellow tunic crisp and uncrumpled, the black leather criss-cross straps and belt over it glinting dazzlingly in the sun.

'Pull up by that constable there,' he said to

273

his driver.

The Sikh grinned.

'You are going to give me in charge for reckless, sahib?' he asked.

'No,' Ghote said, 'I am going to pay you damn' well out of public funds.'

As he took out his wallet and began counting notes, the Sikh brought the taxi to a halt just where the constable stood.

The grizzle-moustached veteran appreciated the situation the moment Ghote explained.

'Very good, Inspector sahib,' he said, 'I will take this fellow to the chowkey just as fast as he can march. There I will telephone *ek dum* to Superintendent Karandikar and tell him it is the paan-shop in Bawoodji Lane. I know it well, their paans have so little in them it is like having a piece of American gum only.'

He laughed with brisk joviality and jerked the wretched Shah out of his seat in the car and on to the pavement. Then, holding his arm in a hair-matted hand that was like an animal clamp, he bustled him unceremoniously away.

Ghote too set off at a fast walk, judging that even with the pavements as crowded as they were it would be quicker to go on foot than get the taxi to drive further on. In a few moments he came to the entrance to Bawoodji Lane and glanced up it.

He thought he could catch a glimpse of the open front of the paan-shop about half way along. He almost expected to see one of the searching squads of uniformed constables noisily barging into it, with little Pidku at the back still unprotected. But in fact there was no one other than the milling everyday throng all along the crowded length of the lane.

He hurried on. And when he came to the next turning he could hardly restrain himself from breaking into a run as he went up along the narrow lane in search of the seemingly blocked passageway the accountant had told him about. Only the thought that a run would draw unnecessary attention and perhaps warn the kidnappers kept him down to walking pace.

People of all sorts, idling, squatting, sleeping, walking, stopping to haggle, stopping to gossip, taking time to revile and curse one another, blocked his way. He barged and pushed past them. He twisted and wriggled. And all the time he kept glancing forwards and back, measuring and estimating the distance he had traversed, calculating how much further he would have to go till he came level with the paan-shop and could expect to find the narrow passageway.

A mooning cow with a vile, slobbery strip of mango peel dangling three-quarters of the way out of its mouth lumbered straight up towards him. He gave it a vicious push and shoved his way past.

And then, just as he had decided that he must have somehow missed seeing the passage, over across on the other side where another lane turned off at a right angle something caught his eye and then sent a thump of joy through him that stopped him dead in his tracks. The whole end of the short, cul-de-sac by-lane was stained a vivid and unlikely blue from the broken stones of its footway to the tops of the dark, tumbling houses on either side.

The wall blocking its end, he decided still joyously, must be in fact the wall of the Holitints factory itself. So the back of the paan-shop on the other side of this lane would be only just within range of the blowing blue powder. And that would be why that finger had had only a few grains of blue under its nail.

So this must be the right spot. And, yes there on the left was the passageway. The sunlight pouring on to the faces of the houses on either side had made it hard to see, but, once spotted, the dark, black slit was impossible to miss.

He did break into a run now. A dog, slinking along by the vile-smelling street drain nosing for something to gnaw at, got under his feet. He nearly fell, recovered and plunged into the passage entrance.

It took him several moments to adjust his eyes to the darkness, which seemed at first almost as thick as night despite the strip of hard blue, sunlit sky above. But at last he was able to make out where he had to go.

Yet when he did so his heart almost failed him. The way ahead seemed totally blocked. There was a tall, battered hen-coop, round which there pecked and squabbled half a dozen dispirited chickens. Beyond that was a mound of indistinguishable rubbish topped by an old barrel with half its side knocked out. The whole was the better part of five feet high.

He remembered, however, what the miserable Shah had said and pressed on. Past the coop he was able to see over the rubbish barrier, and, sure enough, the passageway did continue. He scrambled his way up the mound of rotting ordure, getting his trousers stained appallingly up to and beyond the knees. But he was able to get over, and he staggered gratefully down the last few yards of the passageway.

He came out, as the accountant had said he would, into a small garden, if garden such a dirt-patch could be called, bounded by low, crumbling walls.

Which way to go? He decided that probably he should back-track a little and turned his attention to the low wall on his left. There was no difficulty getting over.

Moving cautiously so as to avoid if possible attracting the attention of any of the people living in the houses on either side, who might well be more in sympathy with the law-breakers than with the forces of order, he crossed the garden he had got into and peered over its far wall. And, yes. Surely, there, two gardens further on, were some soft, springy-looking bundles that might well contain new supplies of betel leaves for the paan-shop.

He hurried on, and at the next wall was able to confirm by the clean, tangy smell cutting over the prevailing low stench that he was indeed within a few yards of his destination.

For a second he stood, crouching so that only his eyes came above the level of the dilapidated wall in front of him, and surveyed the paan-shop garden and the back of the house itself. It did not take him long to find what he first sought: up against the wall of the house there was a small lean-to shelter made from heavy timber.

There must be the place where Pidku was hidden. He hardly blamed the searchers for leaving it out of account. It was only some four feet high and had evidently been built just as a store-place, good enough to keep out the rain. But, confirming to him that what was in it now was valuable indeed, there was on its lid a heavy chunk of broken concrete secured with rough wire. It would quite obviously be a great deal too heavy to be lifted by a boy of five.

With one last glance round to make sure no one seemed to be taking particular interest in his activities, Ghote crossed the remaining distance separating him from the paan-shop's garden. He heaved himself over the last wall and moved rapidly across to the wooden bunker, every step confirming his observation that it was indeed what he had been looking for. When he reached it he saw, as he hoped, that it was only the weight of the broken-edged concrete block that was keeping the close-fitting wooden lid in place.

He shut his eyes for an instant, took a quick, deep breath, clasped the front edge of the thick lid and heaved both it and the wired-on block upwards.

At first the inside of the bunker, which

must have measured about four feet across each way as well as in depth, seemed totally black. But then there was a tiny movement, almost as if a light breeze had disturbed a bit of old rag and had faintly fluttered it.

Ghote bent forward, peering with every degree of force he could bring to his eyeballs. And, yes, there lying at the bottom of the bunker was a child.

But what a child.

As Ghote's eyes grew bit by bit accustomed to the darkness inside the bunker, he was able to make out all the details. Always in his mind's eye he had pictured little Pidku as an attractive boy, a pleasanter pair to Haribhai, chubby and well cared for with glossy hair and a smiling, lively, fragile-skinned face. The only son of a father as devoted as the tailor would have such a boy despite his poverty, he had thought. But the child lying crouched sideways on the earth floor of the bunker, although from the ball of dirty and knotted rag round his right hand he must be beyond doubt little Pidku, was as far removed from the boy of his mind's eye as it was possible to be.

He was no longer dressed in the 'latest fashion, straight from the shops' clothes that he had, so long ago it seemed now, mischievously exchanged with his rich

280

friend, Haribhai. Instead he was naked. And his limbs, that ought to have been rounded and sturdy, seemed scrawny as a half-starved chicken's. He was dirty too. The whole top half of his legs was covered with mess. And the face that looked slowly up to the light, blank with fear, was in no way the face Ghote had so often pictured under the horny hand of the knife-threatening kidnapper. Instead it was grimy, mucus-smeared and already blotched with sores.

Ghote, peering down at the little prince who had hovered at the end of his quest, found that he could not produce the least fraction of that well-springing of joy that ought to have burst from him. Only a very slight feeling of disgust manifested itself at the sight of the repulsive object moving mutely on the messy floor of the bunker.

But this was Pidku. And the paramount thing was to complete his rescue.

Ghote leant well forward into the bunker, ignoring the rancid smell that entered his nostrils like dagger thrusts.

'It is a friend,' he whispered. 'I am going to take you quickly to your Pitaji.'

But there was hardly anything that could be seen as a delighted reaction from the scrawny, apathetic captive at the bottom of the bunker.

'Up we come,' Ghote said, putting all the reassurance he could muster into the words, as he leant further in and slipped his right arm round the boy's terribly small chest.

He lifted him—the burden was disconcertingly light and insubstantial—up and out of the bunker and thankfully closed its heavy lid.

'Now,' he said, 'we must be quiet while we go. It is only over a few walls and along a passage, and then we will be safe.'

Putting his feather-light, precious, dirt-encrusted and offensively smelling burden across his shoulder, he turned and prepared to clamber across the wall beside him.

And it was then that he saw, across the intervening gardens, just emerging from the passageway, a big, bearded man who in the moment that he glimpsed him appeared to have no hands.

CHAPTER SEVENTEEN

The glimpse Ghote had of the bearded man as he looked at him across the gardens between them was extraordinarily clear. And it put into his mind at once and absolutely the conviction that he could be none other than the driver of the car that had taken Haribhai Desai and Pidku, the man Haribhai had described as having no hands.

For a long-seeming moment Ghote stood stock-still, his scrawny burden reversed over his shoulder. And in that instant he was able to work out that, of course, the bearded man was not handless. But he was one-handed. And from the angle he had seen him his one good hand had been hidden, as it must have been too when Haribhai had been briefly in the kidnappers' car.

So the garbled description Haribhai had given in the nursery of the penthouse had unexpectedly served its turn in providing a necessary warning. Ghote quietly and slowly knelt down till he himself and his precious burden were safely concealed under the shelter of the garden wall.

Was this fellow—he would be the Muslim one: Shah had used his name: yes, Mohamed

Israil—was he coming to warn the others that a search party was near again? Hardly. The searchers would have got much further than this from the Holitints factory now. No, more likely he was coming to help them whisk their captive to the new hiding place. Or, would it be to help them to escape leaving the captive to be found dead? In any case before very long he would be in the garden here.

Should he make a bid for escape while there was still a little time? But the chances of getting clear were nil. The Muslim could easily outpace him hampered as he would be by Pidku and would be bound to recognize what his burden was. Could he go forward and dodge past him? The passageway, and the safety of the crowds beyond it, was not so far away. Or could he surprise the fellow and put him out of action?

Possibly, if he was on his own. With Pidku over his shoulder, there was not a hope.

So there was only one thing for it.

'Listen,' he hissed at Pidku, swinging him round and trying to suppress the anxiety he felt. 'Listen, for a little I am going to put you back where you were. But do not worry. Soon we will go.'

It seemed that a faint light of understanding did show in that filthy and sore-blotched face, though the boy said nothing.

Ghote carefully raised his head and saw that the Muslim was busy crossing a wall. With quiet speed he re-opened the bunker and lifted Pidku gently into it. Still the boy did not make a sound.

To lower the heavy lid was quick agony. The thought of darkness closing in again on the captive was almost too much to bear. But it had to be done.

After it, Ghote gave a quick look over towards the Muslim, but it was plain the fellow had spotted nothing amiss. So he hurled himself into the narrow space between the side of the bunker and the garden wall, which he had seen in a flash as a hiding-place and crouched there fighting to control his breathing.

He was not well concealed. He was hardly concealed at all. But provided the Muslim swung himself over this garden wall in the same fashion as he had done with the wall he had been getting across before, then he ought not to see him.

Unless the fellow chose to linger in the garden.

But if he did not, if it passed off safely, what then? If the Muslim went into the house, would it be safe to get Pidku out again and risk making a getaway? How long would it be before the grey-moustached traffic constable got a message to Superintendent Karandikar?

It surely would be some time yet. So if the Muslim did go right into the house—Ghote tensed like a twang-hidden spring as he came over the wall, mercifully bending away from the bunker and with his handless arm swinging high—then he would take the risk and try to make a dash for it with Pidku.

And, yes, he had walked straight over to the door into the house, which lay a little recessed from the wall against which the bunker had been built. The sound of a knocking. Evidently the door must be locked. Tap, tap, tap. Tap, tap. It sounded like a code signal.

Now the door was being opened. That must be the shriek of a tight bolt.

He would give a lot to be able to see exactly what was happening. But he did not dare even peer above the top of the bunker. The house door was not very far back from the wall behind him and the Muslim might easily have stepped away from it to a position from which he could see the bunker itself.

'Ah, it is you, Mohamed.'

The flat voice of the man on the telephone. He was more relaxed here, but there was no mistaking him.

'Yes, it is me. Who else did you think it would be?'

'The car is there?'

'Ready and waiting.'

'I will tell Sudhir. Did you get through to the great Mr Shah this time?'

'They said he was not answering his telephone.'

'Then we will not wait. I will bring Sudhir. We will deal with the boy and then go. After that we can telephone to that paper and tell them where to look for the body.'

'Okay, okay. But hurry.'

Crouching between the side of the bunker and the crumbling garden wall with every muscle taut, Ghote did not need to consider the conversation he had heard. It was all too clear. The three of them were about to make their escape clear away from the danger area, happy that the hunt seemed to have passed them by. They had decided that they would never now get their twenty lakhs from the proprietor of Trust-X and they were going brutally to kill Pidku so as to soften up the parents of a new victim.

And, crouching still, Ghote found that he did not need either to consider what he himself was going to do. He was going to make a fight for it.

He eased himself up centimetre by centimetre, ready to leap clear if he heard the slightest indication that the one-handed Muslim was standing far enough back to see him. But, if he could get fully to his feet unseen, he might perhaps be able to tackle this one antagonist and put him out before the other two got back.

Perhaps then he would stand a chance of getting out of this alive.

He was under no illusion that it was indeed his life that he was about to risk. To take on these men at the very moment they were about to kill for their own profit was, quite simply, courting death or at best being left for dead.

Well, at least it seemed the Muslim must be standing close to the door in a position where he could be taken by surprise.

But the chances of success were minimal still, he knew. Unarmed, to launch himself on to men each of whom was likely to be carrying a weapon and none of whom would hesitate to use it: it was tantamount to flinging himself down a well in suicide.

But it had to be done. He could not sneak away and leave that scrawny, stinking, soiled boy to die.

Because Pidku was the future. He was unproven. He might rise to anything. While he himself had undergone the tests. And he had been proved, like most others in the world, to be mixed metal. There was no choice.

One. Two. Three.

Noiselessly he propelled himself in the direction of the hidden door. If only the big Muslim would turn out to have his back . . .

He checked himself in blank amazement as the door came in sight. There was nobody there.

Immediately the explanation came to him. Simple enough, the Muslim had not waited but had strolled in through the open door. No doubt he had thought the other two had been taking too much time.

What to do? Too risky to try to make a getaway with Pidku. That bunker lid was noisy.

Hide flat up against the wall beside the door so as to gain maximum surprise? That would pay best.

He went quickly over.

From inside the house he could hear muffled voices now. They seemed to be disputing over something. Was one of the other two having last-second doubts? Was he the one who 'still had some heart left'?

Dare he himself risk going for Pidku after all?

No. Footsteps. Hurrying, heavy footsteps. He braced himself.

And then, out into the sunlight of the little, cluttered garden in swift, tiger-like strides there came Superintendent Karandikar.

'No,' he called back loudly. 'No one making off this way.'

He swung round to re-enter the house.

'Sir,' said Inspector Ghote.

'Ghote? What are you doing here, man?'

'You did not get my message, Superintendent sahib?'

'Message? What message?'

'I sent a message by a traffic constable, Superintendent. To say I had discovered where they were keeping Pidku, keeping the kidnapped boy, Superintendent. But I did not think you would be able to get here so soon.'

'I know nothing about any of that, Inspector. And I am none too certain I like your presence here. I was conducting a personal second check on every doubtful building in the area, and the men we found in the back of the house here started to cut up rough. So I knew we had struck gold.'

He swung away and called back into the house again.

'You have found the boy? No harm done, eh?'

'He is here, Superintendent sahib,' Ghote said. 'In here.'

He went over to the bunker and lifted the heavy lid. Superintendent Karandikar came over and peered in beside him at the small, uneasily moving figure down at the bottom.

'Hm,' he grunted dubiously.

He straightened up and took a pace back.

'You had better go and find a telephone and get hold of a police ambulance, Inspector,' he said. 'We will have to get him taken to hospital, if only to see he gets a thorough wash.'

'Yes, sir,' said Ghote.

He put his arm down into the bunker and once more pulled out the scrawny, feather light, unprepossessing bundle that was little Pidku.

'Now everything is all right again,' he said to him.

The boy blinked but did not speak. His face was withdrawn and all his tears had been exhausted long ago.

'Put him down, Inspector, and hurry along,' Superintendent Karandikar said.

'Yes, sir,' Ghote answered. 'Where shall I put?'

The superintendent looked irritatedly from side to side as if expecting a police matron to materialize because he needed her.

'Oh, find somewhere, man,' he said. 'Find somewhere and get to that telephone. We want immediate medical evidence if we are going to make the best case we can in court.'

'Yes, Superintendent.'

Ghote hoisted the silent Pidku on to his shoulder as he had done before and walked in at the back door of the paan-shop. This time, however, he felt a tiny frog-paw of a hand clutching weakly at his shoulder. The faint, feeble sensation warmed him.

But was it only a last flicker of a dying inner fire? Had the kidnappers after all done their worst to little, maimed Pidku, frozen his heart for ever?

Sick with the beginnings of this new fear, he looked round for somebody with whom he could leave the little living enigma he was carrying. But there seemed to be nobody. On one side of the back room of the shop the proprietor, his wife and grown-up daughters were standing in heavy police custody while on the other side the three kidnappers were lined up with their faces to the wall, handcuffs linking wrist to wrist. And, yes, Ghote noted one of the two he had not seen till this moment was wearing a red checked shirt.

He went through to the open-fronted shop itself. A pressing crowd had already collected

292

in the lane outside and two burly constables were keeping them back. He looked at the panorama of faces out there hoping to find one that seemed as if it belonged to a person he could ask to come inside and nurse his terrified-to-numbness charge. But every face showed only avid curiosity.

No doubt, he thought, there are really mothers among them who would warmly enwrap little Pidku, were they taken out of their surroundings now and told his story. Or there would be young girls who would be as kind. Or fathers, or indulgent uncles. But at this moment they were all submerged in that common, hating, sharp desire to know and to crow.

He glanced hurriedly round the shop, spotted a dark, out-of-the-way corner behind the counter and rested little dumb Pidku there, beside a dangling sheet of beaten silver foil hanging down to make wrappings for the occasional luxury paans a shop like this might be asked for.

'Back in a minute,' he said, crouching in front of the little inert body and smiling hard.

Fear-frozen eyes stared back. Not a flicker of response showed in them. Would any ever show?

Ghote heaved himself to his feet and made up his mind simply to be as quick in carrying

293

out Superintendent Karandikar's orders as he could be.

He went past the two guard constables and pushed his way, not without a couple of spurts of petty brutality through the watching crowd. But then, as he turned to look up and down Bawoodji Lane to see if he could spot a shop that might have a telephone, he saw about a hundred and fifty yards away at the distant road junction a vendor with a barrow of toys from which there grew like a bunch of bright flowers a bundle of gas-filled balloons.

He ran at full pelt up the street, and quickly as he could bought the brightest and best of the balloon bunch, a pear-shaped red one that almost said aloud 'Happiness'. He ran equally fast back with it to the shop, barging his way through the crowd, holding his bright offering high above his head and calling out sharply, 'Police, Police.'

In the shop he hurried over to the corner where he had left Pidku. The boy did not seem even to have moved a leg. He was sitting propped beside the sheet of silver foil where he had left him, staring straight ahead.

Ghote squatted in front of him.

'Look,' he said. 'Look.'

He jigged the lustrous red balloon up and down on its string. Pidku's eyes, as if he were

294

hypnotized, went to the bright globe and moved up and down as Ghote jerked on the string.

'Yours,' he said. 'Yours. Take. Take.'

But the tiny, dirt-covered hands lay still on the boy's naked, soiled lap.

'Take,' Ghote said again, leaning forward and urgently crooning the word.

But still five-year-old Pidku made no move, though his eyes were fixed on the balloon where it caught the light pouring in from the sun-filled street. Carefully Ghote put the string into Pidku's uninjured left hand and closed thin, curling fingers round it. But still the boy made no move.

'Now I must go for some minutes more,' Ghote said.

He got up reluctantly but hurried out again, more than a little anxious in case Superintendent Karandikar came out into the shop and found his orders not being instantly obeyed.

Again he pushed through the avid crowd and again looked for a shop from which to telephone. He had in the end to go along to the top of the lane and round the corner before he found anywhere. Then his call took a terribly long time to go through and there were various difficulties to be overcome at the far end before he obtained a firm promise that an ambulance would be sent out at once. 'Tell the driver to report to Superintendent Karandikar in person,' he concluded, recalling with a jet of bitterness the last time he had given a similar instruction—to the laboratory technicians when he had sent the kidnappers' packet for examination despite the superintendent's scorn and had provided, looking back, one of the main clues that had broken the case.

He put down the telephone receiver thoughtfully. And then, as he was about to pay, leave and hurry back to the paan-shop as ordered, another thought came to him.

'No, I will make one more call,' he said to the shop owner.

He began dialling the number of Manibhai Desai's penthouse.

It needed, he found, a little resolution to complete the dialling and listen to the ringing at the far end. The last words he had had from the proprietor of Trust-X had been chill indeed. But no one else could find Pidku's father quickly, and, he had decided, the tailor had to be told about Pidku and to see him with the least possible delay.

But still the idea of talking to Mr Desai and, worse, of having to persuade him to send for the tailor was not pleasant. Yet the tailor had to be told that Pidku had been found. No more than that yet, that Pidku had been found.

The phone rang and rang. He entertained the idea of putting down the receiver and finding someone else to make the call. Would that perhaps be a more effective way even of gaining Manibhai Desai's assistance?

Then abruptly the ringing ceased and the far receiver was picked up.

'Hello.'

It was the proprietor of Trust-X himself. And he sounded angry.

'Mr Desai? It is Inspector Ghote, sir. I am ringing to—'

'Inspector Ghote. Inspector Ghote. Thank God.'

The totally unexpected urgent joy in the voice sent Ghote into a stunned silence.

'Inspector, you are there?'

'Yes, sahib.'

'So many hours without news of that boy, Inspector. And the father is here, and I have seen him. And, listen, Inspector, after all I wish to pay. That boy must be got back.'

The words were an unstoppable gabble.

'Sir. Sir. It is all right. Sir. Sir. He is safe. Safe.'

At last Ghote's increasingly frantic interruptions got home.

'You say he is safe? Little Pidku? He is

297

found? It is true?'

'Yes, sahib. Yes, Mr Desai. Only a few minutes ago he was found. He is alive. He is at least, alive.'

'Then I will tell the tailor. At once. Now. It is marvellous, wonderful.'

Evidently the note of doubt in those last words of his had not penetrated Manibhai Desai's golden glow.

'Sir. Mr Desai.'

'Yes, yes, what is it?'

'Can you bring Pidku's father here now? I am near the place where he was found. Superintendent Karandikar wishes Pidku to go to hospital for a thorough check-up. But if you drive down here straightaway you would most probably catch him before he goes.'

'Yes, yes, I will do that. *Ek dum, ek dum.* What is the address?'

Ghote told him and laid down the telephone receiver, feeling already happier than he had thought he could in all the messiness that the affair seemed to be ending in. He hurried back to the paan-shop.

And, when he had shoved his way through the crowd, which showed no signs of lessening, he found that, down in the dark safe corner where he had put him, Pidku was actually softly and gently playing with the string of the red balloon.

But hardly had he got to his knees in front of him and tried to get from him the hint of an answering smile as he himself grinned and grinned than a sharp voice behind him caused him to scramble awkwardly to his feet.

It was the Commissioner. In the street the crowd had at last dispersed and in their place stood that magnificent, polished car that had appeared equally quietly on the morning it had all begun, at the moment Ghote had slid that daily pay-out of his into the hand of the beggar boy with the withered, no-account stump of a leg.

Then the Commissioner had proved a figure of unexpected warmth. But now things seemed to be different.

'Superintendent Karandikar?' the Commissioner asked brusquely. 'Where is he, man?'

'There—there, sir,' Ghote stammered, pointing like a fool.

Without a word the Commissioner strode into the back of the shop.

Ghote remained standing waiting for him to come out again, not thinking there was anything he would be wanted for but feeling somehow obliged to show himself being on the alert.

The Commissioner was in with Super-intendent Karandikar for a considerable time, and Ghote had opportunities to steal quick glances at Pidku beside him on the floor and to observe that he was at least still minutely jigging the string of the red balloon. But then at last the voices inside grew louder and a moment later the Commissioner came out closely followed by Superintendent Karandikar.

In the shop the Commissioner turned and gave the superintendent what was evidently the last of many handshakes.

'Once again my congratulations,' he said. 'A magnificently planned operation from start to finish and, above all, a magnificently executed piece of pure detection.'

'Thank you, sir,' said Superintendent Karandikar.

The Commissioner turned and hurried out to his waiting, gleaming car. He brushed by Inspector Ghote, standing rigidly to attention, but appeared not to notice him.

But as the car drew away Superintendent Karandikar turned from watching it.

'Ah, there you are, Inspector,' he said sharply to Ghote. 'I was wanting a word with you.'

'Yes, sir?' Ghote said.

'Yes. Well, I have only this to say. As soon as I get back to my desk I am filling in the appropriate notification to you that you are to appear before a Disciplinary Board. Nobody, Inspector, nobody slides out of obeying orders I give him and then goes off on his own sticking his dirty little fingers into my case. Let me tell you now, I am very much inclined to think that your final piece of insubordination in coming here ahead of the proper search party might very well have resulted in the death of that boy. So you and I will meet again shortly, in different circumstances.'

He turned on his heel and re-entered the back of the shop.

Ghote stood letting grey and sullen waves of gloom sweep over him. He hardly noticed any longer the tiny jerky movements that were Pidku playing bit by bit more confidently with the red balloon. He hardly noticed either when the police ambulance arrived outside to be followed almost immediately by Manibhai Desai's familiar big Buick.

He watched with apathy as the ambulance driver bustled through and reported, as ordered, to Superintendent Karandikar.

'Where is the child? Where the devil is the child?' the superintendent demanded, poking his head out again.

'He is here, sir,' Ghote said, turning and lifting Pidku.

'Right, right. Well, you take him off and make sure he gets the examination I ordered straightaway.'

'Yes, sir, Superintendent,' the driver said, clicking his heels in a thunderous salute.

He took Ghote's mute burden from him with stiff precision, turned and walked smartly out into the street, the red balloon still clutched in Pidku's uninjured hand bobbing and bouncing absurdly above him.

Outside, the proprietor of Trust-X stood with the old tailor, the richly-suited, tall figure and the lean-shanked, singlet-darned one side by side. As the ambulance driver waited for his companion to open the back door of their vehicle, Ghote saw the tailor put out a tentative hand to his son and gently touch him.

And then at last Pidku smiled.

It was no great grin, but the small wrinkling round the eyes in that dirt-smeared face was unmistakable. An unfreezing.

Ghote felt his lethargic gloom sliding away like great, stiff cakes of dust under the first rain of the monsoon. The Disciplinary Board lay ahead. It might sentence him to be dismissed from the force, or to be relegated to Traffic Branch. Or, if he put his side of the affair well, he might escape with only a reprimand. But, whatever the outcome, it did

302

not deep-down matter.

What mattered was that Pidku was back where he belonged, in every way. The case had been brought to a conclusion that was satisfactory.